Malcolm Sutton is an award-winning journalist whose work has been published Australia-wide and internationally. He lives in South Australia where he performs as a musician and runs a fringe theatre company that has produced works in London and Adelaide. The Fake Jesus is his first full-length novel.

www.thefakejesus.com

Published September 2021 by Malcolm Sutton
Developed with the assistance of Arts South Australia
Printed by IngramSpark
ISBN: 978-0-6452025-1-9
A catalogue record of this work is available from the National Library of Australia

Cover by Adrian Riggs and Malcolm Sutton

Visit www.thefakejesus.com for more information

THE FAKE JESUS

MALCOLM SUTTON

For the jagged misfits

SATURDAY

I've been awake for two minutes but I can't move. My sheets reek of smoke and the alcohol in my blood. It's hot outside, I'm slippery with sweat, and I can still feel her wet lips, her incisors gently scraping at my skin, the soft sound of her wicked growl muffled within my belly hair.

I feel remnants of passion. I feel like I need a shower. But I want to savour the moment. I want to return to sleep and put her back together, turn back the clock, do it all again, seduce her, fuck her, destroy her, laugh at her, turn my back, feel righteous all over.

When I sleep I dream of Hollywood vampires. Last night one took me to heaven. She was the mistress, the countess, the leader of a flock of female vampires attempting to take over the city, the mall, the endless expanse of alleyways, department stores, billboards, bars and secret clubs of my dreams — all of it beneath a city-wide canopy that enclosed us all.

Last night they were doing what they always do — being bad, trying to take over. I was doing what I always do — joining them under the pretence of wanting to be one, wearing designer clothes, becoming trusted, getting close, then spraying them with wooden shards and stabbing them, bashing them, knocking their heads from side to side so their fangs bust out the side of their faces.

They look at me with hurt, with love, with betrayal. I hit them harder and harder until they are nothing but a pile of bloodied pulp on the asphalt. Saliva runs down my chin. My heart pounds with violent ecstasy. Even as they become nothing but mangled raw sausages leaking over the ground, I kick the mess and scatter it about and push it into a fire.

Then I smile. Then I turn to the Old Man nearby and smile again, and he will congratulate me.

He always does.

Now I lie in my oily bedclothes and attempt to fall asleep again, to return to the moment post-sex before I destroyed them and do it all over, feel it again, at least try and get the leader's name before I wipe her from existence. But I can't do it. I've finished sleeping. The dream floats away and leaves me alone to realise things. Horrible things.

This is not the first time I've woken up today.

Flashbacks from the previous night circle my bruised mind.

'You stupid fucking wanker,' she said. 'Why does everyone do that?'

I remember a rubber band at the Exeter Hotel. Tracey was returning to our table with a pint of beer. I wrapped the rubber band around my fingers, making it a gun, and pointed it at her with a smile. I didn't know it was going to fly off my hand and hit her in the eye. It wasn't my intention to shoot. I was only trying to show affection.

Her face changed as the rubber band collapsed off her face. She stopped for an instant, a nanosecond, before her own smile warped into a blackening pit of rage. *Bang bang bang* went her steps, such acceleration, from zero to seven kilometres-per-hour, *bang bang bang* and then beer over my head, down my neck, into my neckline and down my back. And then *wham*, a pint glass into my temple, falling with a thud to the table where it did not break, a torrent of abuse and she was gone.

'Well,' I said. 'I wasn't expecting that.'

No one laughed but as far as I was concerned it was the perfect line.

The night went on. I got drunk. I played darts with Tracey's friends. I didn't do all that well, but I tried in earnest, sizing up the dartboard, positioning my feet, breathing out and throwing the dart. But I missed altogether and it pissed me off because I had it lined up so well, prepared so thoughtfully. I wondered if I should change my routine. I also wondered why everyone always shot Tracey with a rubber band. It was the first I'd heard of it, or witnessed it, and if that was her reaction to such a common occurrence, shouldn't somebody attach a warning to her face?

At some point one her of friends explained that Tracey's brother did the same thing when she was little, how she couldn't see out her eye for two days.

'Oh,' I said. 'Well that explains that.'

Leanne would never be so violent. Leanne's just a parasite.

I remember how I lost at darts and impulsively pulled the dartboard off the wall, snuck it past the bartenders, and into the beer garden where I placed it beneath a table of drinking 20-somethings.

'I'm just going to leave this here for a while. Don't tell anyone.'

Later on, Tracey's friends asked where the dartboard was. They wanted to play. I remember returning to the beer garden. Faces I don't know are smiling at me. Faces I don't know are laughing at me. They nod towards clusters of tables and chairs and I know it's gone.

'Where's the dartboard?' Tracey's friends ask again later.

'I don't know,' I say. By now I can hardly walk. I think they are annoyed with me but I don't care. I'm at the bar buying another beer. I have a faint memory of a bartender yelling at them, but the dartboard is a distant memory. I'm looking about the bar for a woman, for something to approach as it's time, time for that kind of release.

Tracey's friend, the messenger who explained her violence. I would feel sick now if my stomach wasn't clotting with revulsion. What was I thinking?

She looked wild and I told her so. Her response was to grab everyone and leave.

'Shit,' I say, and roll over on myself. Regret is a disease that covers my skin with hives. But I only went out with Tracey twice, the first by accident — a one-night-stand — the second out of guilt. I hardly knew her. She was just a —

I double up on the bed and grasp my stomach. 'Fuck.'

I remember entering the beer garden again, feeling abandoned, feeling alone, feeling too old. I remember standing up on the 20-somethings' table — their faces reminded me of wet cheese and reality TV — and telling them that their generation was the weakest sack of pus-filled shit I ever had the misfortune to be associated with.

'You're a bunch of phonies, digital cut-outs and fashion slaves,' I said. 'You've got no idea how to party, how to get it on with life, how to care for anything but your emoticon updates, Instagram breakfasts and pointy shoes. If some bastard sprayed anthrax round here like it was hairspray they'd be doing us all a favour.'

And then … then I pulled down my pants and showed them my arse.

Shit.

My self-respect collapses and decadence covers me in mud.

It's not good; it's not glamorous. Decadence is not a sexy actress on a movie set. It's plain. It's everywhere. You will die and nothing you do will ever matter, and people will only grieve that you led such a pathetic life, and once the cancer sets in, once the sickness spreads and takes over your life, you will have no chance to turn back time, to start again. You will die and that will be that.

Sweating upon sheets, the memories circle and I feel like scum, like I'm going to hell, like I've lost all sense of me, who I am, where

I'm from, the family who brought me into the world, the privileges they gave me.

But they're dead now, so what does it matter? And what about last night? There'll be ramifications. People will hate me because the pub won't buy a new dartboard. They'll buy a water feature instead and blame me for ruining everyone's fun. Tracey wanted a third night in my bed. Now she wants to smash my face with a pint glass. There's a bunch of new adults who I'm sure to bump into one night. I spat at them all. They know what my arse looks like. Some of them even know what it smells like. And then ... and then ...

This is not the first time I've woken up today.

I stayed out after the pub closed. I went to Sugar and waited for fresh prey. She had a slightly crooked nose but I liked the feel of her tired arms around my waist. We took a taxi to her house, somewhere out west, some place where she never turned the lights on and a big dog barked out back. We fell onto her bed and I didn't try to screw her. I never have such definitive intent. I like to see what happens, go where it goes, take what is given, give what is wanted.

She asked if I was gay. She asked why I didn't just do her.

'It takes more than a slap and tickle to get me excited,' I said.

She laughed and put more effort into it. We rooted and I fell asleep. Later on there were noises in the dark, someone coughing, someone hacking and wheezing, someone coming from afar to stomp past the bedroom and towards the back of the house. But no lights, no little sliver of a glow from beneath the bedroom door. Just sounds, just water in pipes, and the tread of a sick-sounding stranger returning to the front catacombs of a blackened house.

I had to go. The house held secrets I didn't want to know. But as I crept quietly out of the bedroom and down the hallway, I heard the stranger stirring again, more coughing, the thud of feet onto floorboards. There was a sudden glow from an LED clock appearing before me, its glow peering through a widening crack in the black. I lunged across open space, blindly waving my hands before spotting the dim smear of natural light outlining the front door.

'What the …?' came a guttural voice.

I ran. I hit the wall hard. I searched frantically for a doorhandle.

'Who's there?'

'Don't fucking touch me,' I screamed before finding the handle and wrenching the door ajar.

The groggy dawn was before me. I ran, the sounds of shouting in my wake, a girl's protests, a man's rage.

'My fucking wife!' he bawled.

Now I've done it all. Outside my room it's reaching 34 degrees Celsius and there isn't a cloud in the sky. It's the middle of winter and it hasn't rained in months.

Does it matter if I didn't know she was married?

Reckoning awaits me. Terror licks my feet. The abyss of an endless void yawns and I feel vampires inside waiting to gnaw my dick.

But surely ignorance is bliss?

I roll off my bed and scratch the tattered curtains apart with a sigh.

I look out the dirty window, stunned like a rabbit, unable to take my eyes from a blank spot where I don't see anything at all. Air whistles in and out my sinuses. Then I notice my letterbox. A yellow envelope is sticking out of it. It wasn't there last night, and Australia Post doesn't deliver on Saturdays.

Shit.

Leanne strikes again.

She's probably down the road right now, parked in her car, looking at my house, wondering if I'm asleep, if I'm thinking of her, if I'm dreaming of her, if I'll even notice her parcel.

Her offensive can wait. I need to get up and find something to eat, something to soak up the booze in my gut. I stumble into the living room, stopping to steady myself upon a chair frame as pinpricks of blue light dance in my vision. They are electric. They float upon my pupils and itch with dryness. The carpet is moving. My legs are squishy and full of spaghetti mince. I want to hit the couch and collapse, watch TV in wait of recovery.

If Rupert was here I'd shove the table it used to sit on right up his arse.

'The TVs have eyes,' he cried last Saturday night. 'Inside every one of those screens, a tiny little video camera watching and recording, sending the insides of your house back to Google. It's true, man. The TVs are one-way *glass*. You can't see in but *they* can see out. They're everywhere. They watch all of us, man. They catalogue everyone. They know everything about us, what we do, what we say. Every time we turn on a TV, they turn on too. You know it. But nobody fucking knows, man, 'cause every time you smash a TV, it fries inside and there's nothing left to find.'

He proceeded to hurl a bin through the shopfront window and attack every one of the TVs on display. Biddie and I heard them smash as we fled the scene in terror, and later that night when Rupert returned to us, still pumped up, still gnashing his teeth and spitting saliva every ten seconds, he turned his attention upon *me*, told me *my* TV was evil, declared *my* TV to be the reason I hated my life, alleged *my* TV brainwashed and pacified me, and sent my image back to 'those pricks in the Cloud'.

It went out Biddie's car window sometime before sunrise.

I want nothing more than to retreat to its numb lucidity for the entire afternoon but I'm without its distraction, its escapism.

There's a knock at the front door. My heart stops. My skull sucks at its insides, vacuuming for a substance that's suddenly not there.

There's another knock, and this time it's harder.

'Who is it?' I call, the sound of my voice echoing metallic in the high ceilings and naked plaster of Nan's house.

No one answers.

I hurl my body down the hallway with a stumble, yanking my crowbar from its hook next to the entrance before wrenching the door ajar.

'Hello?' I bark, the crowbar raised above my head ready to strike.

There's no one there, just hot air as unnatural in winter as my feelings are for bedroom vampires. But then I notice him. Barely reaching my knees, a small garden gnome sits on my porch. He looks at me with indelible cheer, his curvy hat and Christmas beard a strange mixture of faded red and orange under the yellow sun of Saturday.

'You used to live out back,' I say.

He smiles in reply.

I step out the door and can hear Leanne's footsteps running away in the distance.

Why the hell would I want the garden gnome back? Why the hell would I ever want to see it again?

'Fuck off,' I say to the ceramic mute, the absurd calling card from a relationship that should have been done and dusted three months ago but instead claws scars of belittlement down my back.

'And stop fucking smiling!'

And now she's won. Now she's heard my voice from the distance and knows I'm home, knows I've answered the door, knows I've seen the letterbox and her yellow parcel in wait.

I march outside and rip Leanne's package from the letterbox so violently it breaks off the fence and clatters to the ground. Election flyers and junk mail spill onto the footpath. 'Vote Labor for progress'; 'Liberals — a stronger economy'; 'Foodland, the mighty South Aussies'.

'It's not yours and it never will be,' I scream at the package in my hand. Then I turn my rage in the direction I heard Leanne run, shutting my eyes lest I see her treacherous frame.

'Fuck off, will you,' I shout. 'Why won't you just leave me alone?'

I retreat inside, throwing Leanne's package onto the carpet and slamming the door before immediately opening it again and swinging the crowbar into the garden gnome. Pieces of its head scatter about the porch with the dull, unsatisfying sound of violated plaster. I step back inside but now Leanne's parcel greets me from the hallway floor.

'Peter', it reads.

She always did make me hate my name. I kick it against the wall a couple times before picking it up and ripping it open. Papers flutter to the ground and I glimpse a few words. 'Adelaide Magistrates Court', reads one. 'Annexure 1 as referred to in the Affidavit of Leanne Tilly', reads another.

I pick up a piece of yellow paper with Leanne's handwriting on it.

I'm sorry it's come to this Peter, the loss of your family, your ongoing guilt and recent loss of your last remaining relative. I can't imagine how that must feel. But I fear it's more than grief. The following are letters that you wrote towards the end of our relationship. They show that you're not okay. They show —

I screw the note up and throw it away. I'm not gonna stand for this. I'm not gonna let her play her twisted, snaky game. She can take her legal claim and shove it right up her —

At that moment Nan's old landline rings.

'Hey man.'

It's Biddie.

'How you going?'

'I'll be there in ten minutes. We're going to the beach.'

'What? No way. I'm … I'm hungover. I need to eat.'

'Well go eat then. You've got ten minutes.'

'Fuck that. I can hardly walk and today already sucks.'

'Nothing a few brewskies can't fix, a bit of a swim. Don't be a girl.'

Shit.

'See you in ten.'

Bastard. But at least it will cool me down.

My boneless legs carry me to the kitchen and I attack a cold pizza. I really do need to eat now. There's no future drinking on an empty stomach.

1:09pm

The problem with Biddie is he's stable. I consider myself an escapist. Biddie considers no such thing. I know for a fact I think too much. My mind churns in a swimming pool of piss. Biddie keeps his under control. He appears as peaceful as Buddha yet it aggravates me because he drinks like a fish.

I look at him now, his profile to me as he downs his third beer in ten minutes. I wonder what he thinks of me on ugly days like today, what I've done, who I've hurt over the years. I wonder if he considers me a bastard who deserves everything that's coming my way.

But Biddie never says a thing about my crimes. They're complicated and Biddie doesn't get deep. He will drink at a beer garden all night, wait for me to pick myself off the ground with cigarette butts stuck to my jeans — drool hanging out my mouth and a circle of disgust standing about trying not to make eye contact — and hand me another drink. He won't ask questions and he won't get sloppy. He drinks harder than all of us yet he never reveals a thing

Stable bastard.

Biddie finishes his beer and gets another one, opening it in stylized James Dean perfection. No hesitation, no spillage. He doesn't even acknowledge I've been gawking at him with a sluggish, slowed down snail brain for over five minutes now.

'Shit, man. I think I'm still drunk.'

He blows air through his nose, drinks more beer. He doesn't turn to face me, just continues to look over the sandy beach at all the gorgeous pigs in shiny new bathers and UV shirts, the Gulf of Saint Vincent a quiet blanket stretching to the horizon before us.

'How old do you reckon that chick is?' I ask.

She strides by laughing with a mobile phone stuck to her ear. Her skin is blemish-free. Her bikini pillows are young, firm and in desperate need of my face.

Biddie doesn't answer.

'She looks around 24, right? But she's not. That chick would be 18 — if you're lucky. They're all adults now, man, even the children. You've gotta be careful.'

'You gotta be careful all the time.'

'That's right. Like last night. I didn't know she was married. She never told *me*.'

'Did the guy see your face?'

'Nup. It was dark, so fucking dark. There were no lights in that place. I could hardly see her pil … '

I stop. Biddie doesn't like hearing the details of use and abuse.

'Then you've got nothing to worry about. What's she going out picking up for anyway?'

'Exactly. That's what I reckon.'

'Fuck it,' he says, and the conversation's over. The trial's been opened, the situation clarified and judgment delivered. Biddie crushes an empty can and the sound sends a shudder down my spine. He grabs a fresh beer.

'Leanne's launched her legal claim. She put her fucking affidavit in my letterbox this morning.'

There is a twitch in his cheeks but he doesn't respond.

'I can't be fucked with it. It's the weekend, right?'

'That's it, man.'

'Don't know what I'm gonna do about all this. I … ah, fuck it.'

I can see relief in his face as I drop the subject.

Nothing complicated for Biddie. No real-life problems to hurt his head thinking about. Just an easy life working for his family, a sensible mortgage split with his dad.

He can see I need to talk but he doesn't want to know about it. Neither do I for that matter, but I don't have a choice. Leanne's determination scratches like oil-devoid cogs in the whirring wound of my brain — constantly, without pause, without mercy.

There's a crack of another beer and even I'm surprised how fast Biddie's drinking today, but then he's handing it to me while gazing over the ocean.

'Cheers, man.' I take it. 'Where's Rupert?'

'Dunno. He was meant to be coming. I went by his house but he wasn't there.'

'Hiding out?'

'Pah, Rupert wouldn't know where to put his dick. He's probably at the Stanleys. I'd ring his mobile if you stupid fucks didn't throw them all away.'

'Ah, you know,' I respond light-heartedly. 'The landlines are better. It's like old times, you know? Whoever's on the other end could be anyone. It's kind of surprising. You get to say "Hello?" like you don't know who it is and stuff.'

He squeezes his beer so it crackles. For an instant I imagine a flock of bats violently attacking my head from behind, getting caught in my hair, flailing about, scratching, screeching, yanking out tendrils and leaving bloodied holes in my scalp.

'Unless you've got a caller display,' he says.

Fuck, I hate the sound of metal.

'Yeah, but I don't, and that's not what it's about, right?'

Biddie doesn't answer. I think of our drive here when I spilled the details about last night. I told him about the rubber band: he laughed. I told him about mooning the 20-somethings: he laughed. I told him about the dark house and the crooked-nosed wife: he winced. Then we sat at the traffic lights for what seemed like hours and said nothing, a blue federal election poster staring at us from a stobie pole — one gaping, white-toothed politician persuading us with his frightening grin to vote for him, vote for his party, vote one.

'Know who you're voting for?' I asked.

'What's the difference?' Biddie responded.

And I wanted to scream because those lights stayed red and there was nothing left to say, no more details of my exploits to transmit, our lack of rapport agitated by the radio commercials that Biddie insisted on tolerating from his car radio. We waited to get to the beach. We waited to get drunk.

'Yeah, well, I like the landlines,' I say with a stammer. 'I can't stand mobiles anymore. They've done my head in.'

I can feel my body shaking.

'They can see where we are all the time, man,' screeched Rupert last month. 'Even when it's turned off. And don't take no weird videos or shots with 'em either. They got access to that. They got access to everything that's on your phone.'

I didn't believe Rupert's rants for a second, but I liked the idea of getting rid of it all the same.

Peter, we need 2 tlk. I'll come round tnite if ur home?

Ru gonna B home today? I could brng lunch if ur willing to cht?

Answer yr phone Peter. Neither of us needs this 2 get ugly, especially not u. Call me pls.

Leanne's finger-prick text messages were driving me mad. We smashed our phones on the road and pissed on their fragments.

'And your phone doesn't have a fucking caller display, does it?' I say, turning upon Biddie, my voice wavering like a pubescent grommet.

Biddie doesn't respond. He just squeezes his beer and pours it down his throat.

'Stop squeezing those fucking cans.'

'What?'

'I can't stand it.'

Biddie shakes his head, drinks his beer and keeps gazing over the sea, the beach, the accumulating mass of consumers taking another unseasonably warm winter's day to visit the beach. There are kids with buckets; there are parents looking at their phones; there are sporty types running on sand between the jetties of Henley Beach and Grange. They're wearing sneakers and for a moment I feel jealous. They look healthy, yet they are pigs. Why wear sneakers when you are on sand? It feels good on the toes.

'Take off your fucking sneakers,' I shout.

'Oi, man,' Biddie gives my shoulder a small hit. 'There are kids around.'

And he's right. Fucking Biddie, always so bloody right and assured in everything he says and does.

I look at him.

'Something on your mind, dear?' Biddie asks, without returning my gaze.

'What the fuck makes you tick, man?'

He sucks air through barely opened lips, exhales again.

'Well that's just it, isn't it, Pete. I don't.'

'What? You don't tick? That's not what I meant.'

'I know that's not what you meant.'

I sit there and wait for him to elaborate, my mind wilting as if under anaesthetic, the beers I drink uniting with those I consumed last night to create a well of slow heat in my belly, fumes rising though the insides of my body, into my arms, consuming my brain, absolving my senses to rotate airless in space.

A minute passes. Nothing happens. Biddie doesn't show evidence of being involved in a conversation. One smooth-white cheek beneath one pair of jet-black sunglasses — who the fuck would know what's going on in that head? Who the fuck could understand? It's like trying to read the mind of Buddha. Buddha sipping from a beer can every 30 seconds.

Stable bastard.

'I don't get it, man.'

Finally, he turns to face me. Whether or not he's making eye contact is another story. I can't see a thing behind his sunglasses.

'You think too much, Pete.'

'What, and you don't think at all?'

'I don't tick.'

I start laughing. It starts way back in the recesses of my head and rattles its way to the frontal lobe, taking over everything in my mind and shaking it. A jackhammer, an autonomous instrument of release, it moves down my throat, into my chest, squeezing my heart, raping my stomach. It implodes and explodes and causes my weak legs to shudder haphazardly.

I look at Biddie again. He's staring at the sea with the faint trace of a smile. He's had the reaction he wanted. The conversation's gone where he wanted, and he's hardly said a thing.

I've gotta stop thinking. I've gotta stop thinking 'cause it makes me tick.

'I've gotta stop ticking. Right, Biddie?'

The bastard hands me a beer.

'Hurry up.'

'Oh, I'll hurry up,' I say as I finish the last and pop the other.

Pop in my mind of sad, sad green eyes with beautiful lashes and horribly crushed faith.

Fuck off, Leanne.

'Gotta be quick to keep up with you. Hey, Biddie? How many you had, you bloody fish?'

Biddie looks down at the pile of empties next to us in the sand.

'Nup. Don't say. Who cares? I'll just catch up anyways.'

And down it goes. Fresh gas and bubbles accost my nose hairs. I drink too fast and start coughing, hard. *Wham wham wham*, each cough a punch in the chest plate, each cough the creator of blue dots swimming in my eyes. The fit goes on longer than it should.

'Shi … it,' I gurgle dryly. 'Wrong … hole.'

More coughing, more punching, tears in my eyes and my beer is on the sand pouring over fine pieces of stardust. The fit finally eases and through watery eyes I see a woman and her two tiny grandchildren sitting on the beach looking at me, her worryingly, the kids with curiosity.

I wave.

'Hi.'

'Your nose is bleeding,' says Biddie at the same moment as I feel warm fluid splatter upon my arms.

The grandmother collects the kids and moves away. I raise my bloodied arm and prepare to wave again.

Biddie hits me in the shoulder.

'Don't, man. Leave them alone.'

Yet my other arm is wiping blood from my upper lip and it's coming fast.

'What about this then, Biddie? What's this all about? I … wait, don't say anything. I drink too much? Right?'

'Shut the fuck up and wipe the blood off yourself. You look like a pig.'

I look at him with astonishment. Then I snort at him, but the action sends blood down my throat. It makes me cough again and out it comes in a violent explosion.

Gore sparkles bright in the midday light.

'Idiot,' Biddie says as he gets up to walk away, precious beers in one hand, his other flicking my slime away.

I collapse onto the sand, breathing, spitting, a bloodied mucus and filth-covered animal. I look up at the sun shining away in its endless drought-inducing misery. Relentless, consuming, heartless, it's suddenly blocked out in shadow as ice cold, bitchin' saltwater splatters over my face.

Biddie stands there with a beer can of ocean. I look at him in shock.

'Well that's just it, isn't it, Biddie? We're all pigs.'

I leap up and run down the beach to splash into the water.

Fuck, it's endless. Fuck, I'm dying. Fuck, where does this all end?

I fall to my knees on the seabed and cling to my dreams, to the Old Man, vampires and easy targets. I want to be sleeping in his dark world of make-believe where I can fight against all that sucks, both literally and dastardly, look into the eyes of the Old Man and feel like I'm on track, feel like I have purpose.

But the Old Man only ever comes near the end, once I've had my fun and it's time to destroy. He's never there at the beginning.

I lay my head back into the water and stare up at the cloudless, hot blue sky.

How do I stop ticking?

The water eddies cool and placid about my head. The sun sits omnipresent above my face.

Lord, if there is a Lord, I wish this could all stop. Is there a Lord, or isn't there a Lord? And if there's a Lord, what drugs is He on to make this so?

Something tickles the hair on my legs.

I float my arms out to either side, daring a supreme entity to fix my life, erase my mind, at least give me a lobotomy, but under the water my legs start to buzz with excitement.

What *is* that?

I get to my feet in the waist-high water and look down at my vibrating knees. My leg hairs stick outwards like horizontal antenna. Humming enters my ears. It drones like the sound of a tiny toy motor car.

Am I about to have a stroke?

Invisible energy swarms about me, enters the pores of my skin. I look at my arms and their hairs are standing upright. A small fish silently appears swimming through my legs. It turns about, hovers beneath the surface and looks at my right knee.

What the hell is going on?

The hum in my ears suddenly intensifies and the fish darts forward to peck at my knee. Its impact creates a powerful click in my brain, a static discharge, before the fish rebounds backwards to stop a small distance away and stare at my leg again.

'Fuck you,' I say.

I feel the hairs on my head lift upwards to the sky. Blood-caked nostril hairs crackle. There's another click as the fish pecks me a second time. This time I feel an afterglow in my knee. It hurts a little, like I've been prodded with a hot needle.

Do we have electric fish in these waters?

As if in answer, the fish hits again, and it hurts, it really hurts. Yet I have the idea it hurts the fish too because it's motionless, floating to the surface on its side, as if stunned, as if dead, yet the drone in my ears is intensifying. The increasing charge of what feels like misplaced electricity is enveloping my entire being, and those hairs on my legs are now titanium threads.

The little fish's body floats against my upper thigh and zaps me again.

'Ouch.'

It's time to move. My brain is short-circuiting. I don't know if this is real or not. I hate alcohol. I hate being drunk. I hate being awake.

'Biddie …' I shout as I lift a foot and glance towards him, but he's looking down the beach. Excruciating pain clamps my ankle, serrated tin snips supercharged with a 12-volt car battery. When I lift my foot there's a blue swimmer crab attached.

'Bastard,' I say and flick my foot haphazardly to fall back into the water where a succession of five or so super loud clicks burst in my ears. At the same time five or so needles poke into my thigh, my lower back, my buttocks, my feet.

'Idiot,' Biddie repeats in my head.

I get to my feet and lurch towards the shore 10 metres away, my hair crackling as water cascades from it, my arm hairs flinging droplets away as they stand ever more rigid, my teeth now hurting and wanting to clamp against each other while my tongue expands and tries to push my tonsils into the bottom of my neck. Yet with each push against the water's surface there's a buzz against my skin. With each move of my legs there's a click and a stab and a clamp. I look down and there's an entire school of fish of different shapes, sizes, colours and kinds writhing about my legs, pecking me and pecking each other. Crab claws poke up from within their midst to snap at them before reaching for me as I splash past. Dead or comatose fish bodies float into my thighs.

I hear a girl scream from nearby but then the buzz of that toy motor car in my head roars into a full-sized V8. A huge shape appears to glide ominously in front of me the length and breadth of a surfboard.

'Fucking hell,' I say with a vibrating voice.

A fucking shark!

'Biddie!' I shout but he's not looking at me. He's standing up, looking towards the jetty. There are sounds of kids screaming, someone's mother yelping.

I make another lunge for the shore, feeling all the slimy scaly bodies slithering across my skin, buzzing and rustling as they go, hurting and stabbing, and I hope and pray that I don't step on a stingray.

I don't. Nor do I die. I make it to dry land, turn and look back at an ocean that's coughed me out in a mixture of scales, cartilage and wriggling absurdity.

It's as if an invisible net has dragged every sea creature to shore. They breach the surface, twist, fight and bite, and even from the sand I can hear the crackles, the static discharges. At the same time I notice my body is no longer humming like an electrical wire. The hairs on my legs, arms and head are flat again. Blood from cuts on my feet trickles over wet sand into the water.

A crowd of people run to and from the sea, pulling children out of the water, pulling the elderly onto their feet, consoling the traumatised, placating the wails of infants. Others record the scene with smartphones, standing like sentries as people rush about them.

Thank God it's not just me. Thank God it's not just my head. But what the hell is going on?

Before I can pull my head from confusion, however, the screaming suddenly stops. Everybody hushes one another. The water sizzles with frying fish, yet on the shore humans grow still. Little sobs escape from the mouths of kids. Their parents shoosh them and point towards the jetty 40 metres along the beach. I follow their gaze and see a piercing, blinding light in the barely discernible shape of a man.

A man in white.

"The following note was stuck with a table fork to the front door of the disputed house by Peter Mackay one day after separation." LT

What's wrong with ME? You just keep asking what's wrong with ME? All my speeches, all my rants, all these ridiculous fucking LETTERS, it confounds me that you still don't know.

You're an EXPLODING fart, Leanne, a sum of parts shouting to the world why it doesn't have room for me. Yes, I still dream of vampires. They're so pretty yet so corrupt. I still do them and kill them before they kill me and eat me. That's fucked up, right? And yes, I still dream of the Old Man. He walks around with fire in his eyes like a KNIGHT, but he isn't real and that's FUCKING DISAPPOINTING.

You tell me to put faith in the Universe. You argue that God's tangible. Tell me, Leanne, how does one put faith in a MasterCard? Because your world isn't sustainable. It's death by barcodes, and your crying isn't CLEAN. It's OIL at the end of the line. And if your life is the path to TRUTH then I may as well die right now because everything you've seen and everyone you've known and the air you've breathed and the path you've walked and the jobs you've had and the hope you've felt and the fear

you've had and the joy you REMEMBER and the
deserving attitude you declare on soils
above foundations crumbling ever away
into the molten lava of infinite and
nothingness below, all of it, your entire
existence, pure or otherwise, innocent or
snake-like, dastardly or pro-active, is
nothing more but one huge, deadly,
RIDICULOUS, environmentally CATACLYSMIC,
pissant delusional, deceptively hideous,
horribly clear and obvious-in-all-the-
details of a 21st century BITCHING
information age, mistake.

The world's gonna die now, before our
time is due, and it always fucking was.

I'm done. I've changed the locks.

Off you fuck.

1:35pm

The dazzling spectre strides along the jetty towards shore, his hair brown and long, his beard full, his white robe flapping about like a radiant flag. All about him on the beach people stand and stare. Children stop sobbing and gaze. The water beneath him breaks and whirls about the jetty pylons. Fins burst to the surface and disappear in splashes of silver light. In comparison to the man in white, however, they are as dull as gun metal.

In a daze I turn to look up the beach at Biddie, but he's standing directly behind me. I've inadvertently returned to his presence. He's got a beer in his hand, but he's not drinking it. He's gawking like everyone else and I see reflections of white light in his black sunglasses.

'What *is* thi —

Biddie hushes me like an elder.

The figure is now halfway along the jetty. His blinding eminence is diminishing and I can see his expression. It's one of smiles, of slightly smug-looking self-importance. He raises his arms with his palms in the air and from his mouth comes a loud, deep, forceful voice. It travels as if amplified 20 times, rocking my mind with power and startling the gaping crowd.

Everyone seems to jump and waver on their feet at once.

'Behold, my children. It is I.'

He lowers his arms again and keeps walking towards the shore.

Biddie hits my arm. 'Go get my camera, man,' he hisses, dangling a set of car keys in my face.

'What?'

'In the glove box. There's a video camera. Hurry!'

On the beach, a child resumes crying, and then another. Their little voices fill the stunned air as the white figure turns to look upon those below him on the sand.

His gaze passes over us. I step backwards.

'There is no need to be afraid, my children. There is no need to ever feel afraid again.'

A woman begins to sob. Her husband holds her and puts his shaking hands to her face. 'Hallelujah,' someone else yelps. Another man claps and starts to shriek before jamming his fingers into his mouth with rabid, fretful excitement.

The figure laughs and the sound thunders across the beach. An old lady falls to her knees whereupon a stack of people do the same. I feel momentarily repulsed, a sensation of being surrounded by movie extras and overblown emotion.

The figure draws closer to shore, his features becoming clearer, his face overly human, overly symmetrical, without blemish, white teeth as perfect as a TV news presenter's. But his voice is supernaturally loud, the fish are washing up dead, and Biddie's hitting my arm again.

'Quick. Get my camera!'

'Just use your phone.'

'I … didn't bring it.'

'Ha!' I laugh, pointing at him. 'You got rid of yours too.'

The stable bastard's bottom lip tightens but he refuses to look at me.

'Hurry up.'

I take the keys and jog up the beach towards the car park, away from the spectacle, away from the strangeness upon this usually plain and painfully predictable suburban beach.

'Do not come close to me. I have travelled far, my children, and require space.'

I glance backwards and see that the people have overcome their shock. They're filming with their own phones, uploading footage to social media, to Facebook, Instagram. Some shuffle towards the approaching figure, who stops near the jetty's entrance and waits for them to halt.

I break into a run and scoot up the sandy ramp, through the dunes, onto the lawns and car park beyond where others are moving quickly to the beach.

'What is it?' somebody says.

'Is it for the election?'

'What about our lunch order?'

They flock urgently like sheep, yet they don't know what they're flocking to. I don't know either but I want to get back there all the same.

'Please, stand back, my children,' the man bellows from the beach. 'Allow me to pass through. We'll all speak in good time.'

His laughter hurls across space, shaking me again with its volume, yet once again filling me with a peculiar revulsion.

I reach Biddie's car and retrieve an old camcorder from the glove box. From over the dunes I hear people talking, laughing, murmuring excitedly like a group of people waiting at a rock concert.

Dammit, but I'm missing out.

I sprint back to the scene, ignoring the sign ordering us to use the ramp down to the beach, making a shortcut through the dunes, jumping a little fence, running back to where this man emerged from the ocean with millions of fish and a shining white frock.

'Jesus,' I hear a girl's voice calling. 'Come back, we love you.'

Shit. He's leaving already. Fucking Biddie.

'My Lord,' cries a man's voice. 'We'll wait here for you.'

I bound down a sand dune into a depression, one mound from the beach, Biddie's keys clanging noisily in my hand, scratching against his camera. Not that I care. Not that I give a shit. Why I had to be the one to fetch it I'll never —

The white man is standing alone at the bottom of the basin, tapping his ear, frowning impatiently. He looks up, startled, as I land abruptly on the sand and fall to avoid a collision.

'Crap, man. I didn't see your —

I stop. Don't swear in front of Jesus.

He takes his hand quickly from his ear and smiles unconvincingly.

'It is okay, my son.'

In the privacy of our sandy crater, his voice is small, quiet, and much like my own. It has none of the booming decibels it deployed on the beach. His appearance too has lost its dazzling appeal. There's no shining light in here, no flapping fish. He's just a guy, dressed in a white robe, with perfect teeth.

I get to my feet and shake the sand from my hair.

'What are you doing in here?'

'Please leave me, my son. I must confer with our Father for a moment.'

'My name's Pete,' I say. 'What's yours?'

A surprised cough erupts from his face before he stifles it with a smile. 'Son, please. I'm the son of God, and I …

He tapers off as the hiss leaving my mouth unsettles him.

'Fake.'

He tries to recover.

'Please, son. Give me a moment here, and all will be —

'Your voice sounds normal in here,' I whisper.

'Wh … what?'

'Fake.'

My fingers flex at my sides, clench into a fist. His brown eyes dart to and fro and above me, over my clothes and finally into my own. His eyes widen, and then quickly narrow again, fixating in an obvious attempt to intimidate. But my teeth are tiny batteries breaking open in my mouth, leaking chemicals onto my tongue.

'My son,' he says with another attempt at authority. 'You must return to the beach at once to await me.'

I can hear my gums sizzling.

'Look, mate. I must have a moment to speak with my Father before —

'Pig!'

The word smites the air about us, cuts him off.

'What did you —

My fist flings out and smashes into the side of his jaw so he falls to the ground.

'Fucking pig is what I fucking said you fucking *fake*!'

I drop Biddie's gear and leap onto the imposter, grab his collar and start shaking his head.

'Who the fuck do you think you are? Who the fuck do you think you fucking are?'

Rage heats my bone marrow. Acid flies from my teeth, stinging his astonished and terrified eyes. His hand reaches at his ear, taps and pulls at it. I shake his head again and slam it into the sand.

'How dare you, motherfucker!'

Anger surges from my gut, twisting like a blender, throwing out sputum in sadistic, sticky death graffiti — years of tragedy and abandonment splattering against the interior of my ribcage.

I punch him in the nose. It cracks open and blood cascades into his brown hair.

'You treacherous fucking snake. How dare you? How fucking dare you?'

'Wait … wait,' he says. 'I'm Jesus! You can't do this. I'll cast you into hellfire pits of —

I want to reach into his mouth and down his throat, pull out his tonsils, his heart, his lungs, his liver, and fling them over the crowd. I want the Hollywood vampires of my dreams to smell the flesh and descend upon his entrails, devour each and every one of the pig-fucking bastards they cover, destroy anyone waiting obediently for this prick to re-emerge and fool them further.

I grab his throat and lift his head from the ground.

'I'm going to fucking kill you. I'm going to fucking —

'Please, Jesus. Don't make us wait any longer.' It's the girl's voice again and she's close, on the other side of the dune. 'You've only just arrived. What are you doing?'

The crowd shouts for her to come back.

'Wait,' they call, they order from the beach: happily, safely, obediently. 'He told us to remain here.'

He turns his head towards them and screams.

'Help!'

'Fuck,' I say.

'Jesus?' asks the bewildered girl's voice, even closer.

'Help me, my child,' he screams again before my knee falls down upon his jaw and crushes his face into the sand.

'What's happen … Oh, my gosh.'

I pull my snarl from his battered face and look up to the dune's summit. A teenage girl is looking at us with astonishment. Her expression changes from bewilderment to anger as she realises what I'm doing.

I realise what I'm doing.

'Fuck,' I say again.

But his crime antagonises like a needle-nosed missile. I look at his face and see war, personal war.

Gathering Biddie's camera and keys, I grab the man's hair and begin pulling him back up the sandy incline, away from the girl, away from the crowd on the beach.

'Help!' the girl starts screaming. 'Someone's beating up Jesus.'

The fake Jesus struggles and tries to hit at my legs. I yank his hair and up he comes, wailing in misery, leaving a trail of blood from his broken nose upon the sand.

The sight hits me between the eyes: scarlet upon white, bloodstains on purity.

My stomach shrivels. My sense of self crumbles. I nearly keel over as echoes from hospital corridors reverberate rubberised in my ears, but the girl screams. The unseen crowd shouts. My heart pounds. The heat of the moment sucks in the haunting of my youth and I manage to stumble over the dunes and across the lawns, pulling my fiendish catch in tow. He tries to stop again. I punch his chest. He sways on his feet and I kick him towards the abandoned car park, while the girl follows at a fearful distance, now on the lawns, now waving her hands to the crowd behind and shouting.

'Help,' she screams.

We reach Biddie's car and I open the boot.

'Get in, motherfucker.'

'No way, please, don't do this to me. It is unnecessary … my son.'

I hit him again and push him into the boot. The crowd arrives from over the dunes. They see me close it upon his struggling arms. Large blokes and angry women sprint towards me. I race around the car and leap into the driver's seat.

A scattered whiplash called Biddie pokes into my blistering mind. 'Shut the fuck up and wipe the blood off yourself. You look like a pig.'

The fake Jesus pounds on the boot, kicks the back seats. Muffled shouts bounce off the car as two men reach us and crash against the door. I lock it. They bang the glass. More people arrive and pound upon the boot. The crowd descends like human seagulls and surround me.

'Sorry, Biddie. I'm taking your car.'

I turn the ignition, put my foot down and clip the leg of a tall skinny guy with glasses.

'Out of the fucking way,' I scream, pushing forward into the bleating mass.

Audio advertising blares at me from Biddie's car radio. 'Why shop in the city where there's no shade and little parking?' asks a woman's incredulous voice. 'With two stories of air-conditioned stores and undercover parking, SA's largest shopping mall has —

I hit the radio and look up to see two young men in low cut V-necked T-shirts leap out my way.

'That's it,' I growl through grinding teeth. 'Get in the way and I'll fucking hurt you.'

'You're a dickhead, Peter,' Biddie responds in my head.

'Beach towels, sun shades, umbrellas — hot weather brings hot prices to —

'Fuck off, ' I shout, punching the radio so it sputters. Projectiles of rubbish scatter upon the rear window as I accelerate through the car park, Biddie's engine roaring malevolently, scarlet memories hammering my senses, radio clatter harassing me.

'South Australian baby boomers have been targeted in an election pledge to increase dementia research funding,' a male newsreader says. 'Declaring our population to be the second oldest in the country —

I punch the radio repeatedly until it changes to white noise. In the mirror I see people standing helpless, others shouting abuse, mouths chattering at speed into mobile phones, some holding them upwards to record me digitally, others turning to run back to their own cars, presumably to give chase.

They won't be catching me though. I've left the park at 90 kilometres per hour, skidding right at a T-junction before merging to attack the traffic — but it's lethargic. I react by honking and flashing high beams, overtaking slow cars that turn and halt sporadically against the side of the road, lurching up onto footpaths as they veer to avoid my raging assault. I yank Biddie's steering wheel to the left, turning the car east onto an arterial road, back towards the city, back towards my house. I make another turn, careering right, swinging left, then right again, all the time veering around other cars and pedestrians, all of whom jump out the way or hit their brakes or shout in anger.

I continue like this for a full five minutes, snaking my way through the suburbs, overlooked by white-toothed politicians on federal election posters, zip-tied to stobie poles and front fences, a parade of salespeople promising to fix the deteriorating brains of baby boomers, while dread grows in my belly, gathers weight, threatens ramifications, presents an image of Biddie's agitated face to poke sparklers into my brain, culpability preparing to hit like a train and make me think, make me feel, make me remember — doom and gloom for all I do smashing into my jaw with the impact of a gaol sentence — while the fake Jesus screams and thumps in the boot. My heart pumps and shudders in my ears. I will pay for everything. It's inevitable, but I must keep going until I'm sure I've lost any pursuers, sure no one will be able to track me, sure I've escaped certain death.

I drive recklessly at speed before hitting another main road, slowing down and attempting to travel law abidingly with all the other cars doing the same thing, labouring along at 60kph. I start breathing again. I start thinking again. I start wondering just what in the hell I'm going to do next.

'I am Jesus and you should stop what you are doing right now and ask for forgiveness,' demands the muffled voice from inside the boot.

'I am Pete and if you don't shut the fuck up I'll drive us both off a cliff.'

But I won't do that. I need to calm down. I need to rationalise. I need to understand why the hell I just did what I did. I need to tick. I need Biddie and one of his curt responses. I could do with one of his beers, but the beach crowd will pull me to pieces. Children will kick my eyeballs around. Their parents will cheer and throw in my spleen.

How the hell did they get those fish to flip?

My brain winds tighter and starts to spin, begins to shudder, pinpricks of retinal distortion imploding to scatter across my eyes. The car starts to accelerate again. The speed of my mind inadvertently influences the weight of my foot. I overtake cars, change lanes haphazardly, push through traffic, get abused, but I don't care. I should see Rupert. This shit's right up his alley. If he's not at home, Rupert will be at the Stanleys. The Stanleys live in the foothills, in Blackwood. That's at least 25 minutes from here and my heart is a cartoon boiler. It shakes like dirty machinery and I don't want it to hit redline.

Fucking calm down, man.

But there's no hope. No point. No reason. I'm driving a beaten up prisoner dressed as Jesus in the boot, and I've stolen my friend's car and left him on the beach with a bunch of people who want to kill me kill me kill me kill me kill me.

'Relax, Peter.' Flash in my face of supple skin and tears falling soft like coral spawn.

Don't say my name like that, Leanne.

'Excuse me,' says a muffled voice from the boot.

'Shut up! I have to think.'

'You think too much,' Biddie reminds me from behind his sunglasses.

'Just calm down, young man. There's no need for —

'Look —' I start, but I do have to calm down. I have to rationalise. I need help. I had better ring the Stanleys.

Taking deep breaths, urging my stubborn foot off the accelerator, I slow the car and start looking along the side of the road for a phone box. There isn't a phone in sight.

'Have you got a phone, arsewipe?'

'Wha …'

'Mobile phone, dickhead! You know, convenience, portability, digital connectivity? You got one in that stupid white robe of yours or don't you even have pockets?'

'My son,' he says after a moment's silence. 'I have no need for the contraptions of man. Now, I seriously suggest you pull this car over and let me out before the consequences upon you are everlasting.'

I slam on the brakes and jack-knife the car to a shuddering halt. Cars honk their horns and accelerate around me. I leap out of the driver's seat into an oncoming truck that swerves dangerously into the far lane, its air horns blaring.

Striding around to the boot, I launch it open.

A curled up figure looks up to find my face with difficulty, eyes readjusting to midday sun during the longest, hottest, most terrifying winter of drought this country's ever experienced.

'Now,' he says, starting to get up. 'We are getting some —

My fist comes down hard upon his mouth and I feel teeth break. He slumps back into the boot, out cold, and I slam the lid back down.

"The following abuse was left for me by Peter Mackay on our dining room table two days before separation." LT

Maybe it's a City of CONSUMERS, Leanne. Maybe it's a City of FACTORY ordered shopping malls dumped on your face, your heart, that little café where we first had a COFFEE after Uni and you thought I was a CATCH. You're so clever, you said. You're so smart. I wish I had YOUR MIND. But look at me now, all spooked and MESSED UP in the City of Plastic Lives.

You say it's not too late to get help. You say NAN would hate to see me WASTE MY MIND. But tell me, Leanne, please. What exactly am I wasting? We're on the way out. The river's drying. Forests are burning. Petrol prices are RISING. Little wars are breaking out all over the world, but they're not wars, they're debt collection, and it's not drought, it's CLIMATE CHANGE, and all your talk about houses, careers, barbecues — a frenzied renegade exodus from decency into wet credit cards and Instagram hits — means nothing, contributes nothing, achieves nothing. It's cheap, Leanne. It's ugly, Leanne. We live in a City of Certain Lives. We have snouts but we BAA like SHEEP, lined up like VAMPIRE MEAT. I don't care about your career, and fuck what you say about Nan. You wear her love like a badge.

I want you to move out for a few days. I need some time to myself. I'll be back home tomorrow and you need to be somewhere else.

Forty minutes and two longnecks from the bottle-o later, I feel better. Along with the beer, the lack of protest from the boot has helped to steady my nerves and, even now, parked upon the Stanleys' front lawn, my captive remains silent.

I must have hit him harder than I thought.

'Hey man. How's it going?'

A face of drugged idiocy and a wet smile to match, Rupert stumbles towards me and traces one hand over the roof of Biddie's car.

'You got a new car, man!'

'Nah, this is Biddie's car.'

A tiny frown crinkles his forehead for a moment before his smile returns.

'Oh, yeah. 'Course it is.' Another pause. 'Hey, Biddie's looking for you. What you got his car for?'

'Is he? What, did he ring here?'

'Yeah, man. Biddie's been calling all *day*.'

'I only left him an hour ago. When did you start drinking?'

'Shit, Pete,' he laughs. 'I don't know, about Thursday.'

I look behind Rupert to the Stanleys' front porch. There's a couple of empty spirit bottles and an ashtray sitting next to a solitary chair.

'What? You've been here all that time?'

'Nah, man,' Rupert says, eyes widening with the concentrated look of someone doing their best to lie. 'I've been all over the place. I'm just staying here for a few days, getting a change of scenery.'

'What about your mum?'

He sways and the expression changes to that of a sly drunk who's been caught doing something they shouldn't.

'What about her?' he shrugs. 'She's available, give her a call.'

'Rupert, man, I've got a problem.'

'That's alright, she'll understand.'

'No, fuck ya, I've got a serious problem.'

'Well, I reckon she'll have lotions for that.'

'Rupert,' I shout.

He lurches backwards in slow motion on stationary feet before rallying forward. A rubber man, a gymnastic freak, Rupert's muscles are stretched and athletic from his endless state of wired mistrust.

'Seriously, man. I've got a problem.'

His eyes find focus and light up as they see the desperation in my face.

'Yeah, I know. You've stolen Biddie's car and he's pissed.'

My heart sinks.

'Why don't you come inside? Stanleys are here. They'll let you use their phone. You can turn yourself in to the police.'

'What?'

'But don't mention my name. You haven't seen me and I'm not here. Actually, you're not here either. You can call 'em from here and then go. Actually, maybe you shouldn't call 'em from here. They could trace you. Yeah, don't call 'em from here.'

'Rupert, for fuck's sake, I'm not gonna turn myself in to the cops. What the hell for?'

'Biddie's real pissed off with you.'

'And … stop telling me that. I know he's pissed off with me. But I haven't stolen his car. I'm … I'm borrowing it.'

'What for?'

'Because … well, fuck it. That's not the point. I've got a problem.'

'Hey, man, alright, okay? You got a problem. I got a problem. We've all got problems. It doesn't mean you can go and shout at me, man. I gotta worry about my own things and shit. You gotta chill out.'

Behind Rupert I see a massive shadow loitering behind the closed screen door on the porch. Rupert turns to follow my gaze and sees it for himself, before looking back at me with a hard look, trying to convey seriousness.

'You gotta chill out around here, man. Okay?'

I nod.

'You wanna come in for a drink?'

'I can't. Can you keep your mouth shut if I show you something?'

'I said my mum's got some lotions, not me.'

'Fuck off, Rupert.'

He laughs, walks around to the passenger door and jumps into the car with me.

'Fuck Biddie,' he says. 'Let's go for a drive in his car.'

'I can't take it out on the roads. It's too risky.'

'Why not? You drunk?'

'Not very.'

'Then what?' Rupert looks at me with curiosity.

'Do you believe in God, man?'

'What?'

'Like, are you a religious person?'

'What kind of serious shit have you been doing?' he says, eyeballing me closely.

'Just answer me, motherfucker.'

'Yeah, I believe in God.'

'Seriously?'

'Yeah, so what? You wait till you're about to die, man, then you'll start believing. I swear it to ya. You'll be on your knees shit scared 'cause you're about to cark it into the great unknown. You'll start praying like every other chicken shit in this world.'

I remain silent.

'It's true, man. It happened to me. I cried like a little kid when I thought I was gonna die.'

Scarlet memories burst into my head again. I push them away with a shudder.

'Rupert, you think you're gonna die just about every weekend.'

'It's a dangerous world.'

'But you never are.'

'Doesn't matter. If I think I'm gonna die then it's real and that's real enough. You wait, man. You wait 'til that darkness comes over ya, when you think it's all gonna stop, when you know you're never gonna do a thing again, then you'll see. You'll see like me. You'll —'

'Alright, man. I get it.'

'You ain't no atheist.'

'Never said I was.'

'You ain't no one in the know. You can't tell me I'm wrong.'

'Never said you were.'

'You can't ask me if I believe in God and then diss me when I say I do.'

'Rupert, I didn't.'

'It's not right, man. It's fucking arrogant, that's what it is.'

'Rupert, for fuck's sake, listen to me.'

'Yeah, well, you just show some respect, man. You just show some respect.'

I sigh. Rupert's useless when he's drunk. It's best to suffer his convictions.

'Alright, man. I'm sorry.'

'Really?' He brightens up.

'Seriously.'

I pause. 'What about Jesus?'

'Huh?'

'Do you believe in Jesus?'

Rupert places his hand on his chin and displays a pose of serious contemplation, no doubt relishing that I've engaged him on weighty matters.

This could go on for ages.

'Christianity?' I prod.

'What?'

'Like, the Bible and all that. You believe in God. Do you believe in Jesus?'

'Hmm, I don't know, man. I don't go to church if that's what you're —

'I know you don't fucking go to church. That's not what I'm asking. I'm asking if you believe in —

'There you go again. Disrespect, man. You come here asking me some deep and meaningful shit, and you wanna answer for me. Fuck this.'

He puts his hand on the door handle and pulls it open.

'No, Rupert. I didn't mean it like that.'

He starts climbing out of the car.

'Rupert, just wait. Ah, fuck it.'

I pull a lever under the dashboard and pop the boot. 'Go look in the boot. No, wait.'

He watches me warily.

I get out the car and look at the row of houses across the road. No one's there. I walk in fast circles about the Stanleys' front yard and look over its fences for lurking neighbours: nobody's there. I look up at the porch: the shadow behind the screen has gone and I can hear the sounds of a computer game inside. I return to stand at

Biddie's car where Rupert is watching me with wide eyes from the passenger seat, his posture taut like a wooden mannequin.

'What you doing, man? Why you looking around everywhere? Who you looking for?' He spits outside the door. 'What's your problem, man?' He spits again. 'What you come here for?' He starts running his hands through his hair. 'Fucking hell, man. You shouldn't have come here. You shouldn't have come at all.'

'Just look in the boot, man. It's safe.'

'Safe? I don't know what's safe about you at all, man. What you looking for? What you done? You should just get going, hey?'

Dammit. I should have been more careful. I've wound up Rupert's paranoia like a coiled spring. I can't show him the fake Jesus now. He won't stop bouncing for days. I step backwards and push the boot lid closed.

'Hey, man,' I say brightly, trying to switch his focus. 'You wanna drink? You guys got something to drink in there?' I look at the empty bottles on the porch. 'Or anything left?'

'I don't know, man. I don't know.' Rupert mashes his teeth together and looks steadfastly out the front windscreen to nowhere.

'I'll be back in a moment.' I reach in and take the keys from the ignition. 'I'll get you something. Scotch and Coke?'

'You shouldn't be doing anything, man,' Rupert replies without taking his eyes from the windscreen.

I turn and walk up the steps to the Stanleys' porch. Pieces of peeled paint from the fibro wall litter the concrete. Spider webs decorate the dirty windows. Behind the screen door someone's playing that computer game at full volume. I put my hand on the greasy handle but stop. The Stanleys are hostile. They're only friendly to those within their inner circle, or those who want to buy drugs. I've never been either.

I jump back off the porch and return to Biddie's car.

'Jesus was a great man,' Rupert says, looking up at me with glazed eyes. 'He was the original rebel, man. He came into that place and messed with 'em all, messed with the system, screwed up their politics. He's like the first ever revolutionary. He was a king, man, and did you see that movie? He took the flogging from hell for it.'

Rupert returns his gaze to the front windscreen.

'He was a great man.'

I hang back from the window and wait for him to say something else. Being half sober around Rupert doesn't work. The guy's in a zone and I don't have the drunken advantage to understand it, or even join it, but there's nowhere else to go.

'Hey, man. Have you got anything to drink in there or not? I don't wanna go in and just start looking.'

Rupert abruptly jumps from the car.

'Shit yeah, man. We've got too much. Come inside.'

He bounds up the porch and disappears through the screen door. I glance quickly at the car boot before following Rupert inside.

2:43pm

I'm greeted with cheap floorboards and the smell of dope. A Stanley sits with his back to me in an enclave of fake leather furniture. Light beams radiate from a 4K TV screen and scatter about his bald head. The silhouette of his dome flickers on the wall behind me with sounds of shooting, screaming, and splattering sprite blood.

Rupert's nowhere in sight. The bastard has disappeared into some other section of the house.

I want to say hello to the dome but I don't know which of the Stanleys this is. It will be an issue if I get it wrong. It will also be foolhardy to just stand here without acknowledging my host.

'Hey man,' I offer, approaching the brute.

The Stanley grunts, hands working furiously at his wireless game controller, eyes fixed intensely on the screen, air passing in and out of his lungs. He's a giant plugged into a cyborg connection circular with the TV, his console and wireless controller.

'What's this?' I say, feigning interest in the computer game.

The Stanley mumbles something but I can't hear it over the wicked noise of the violence.

'Where's your bro?' I sit in an armchair that's even oilier than the screen door, hoping he'll answer with his brother's name. It might help to jog my memory.

The Stanley swings his head backwards without saying a word.

'Right,' I say.

The television vomits a green hue over the Stanley's shiny scalp, his thick arms, his blemish-free face. His black eyes suck it in without a trace of reflection. He looks like a fat-necked villain from a comic book, massive torso, oversized head, huge fists and hairless face, but he's a Stanley, one of two quiet, large, identical twin monsters who don't have any family.

It should have made us allies. But it never has, and I've never questioned why. You have to be careful with the Stanleys. It's too easy to get on their bad side.

They came to Blackwood High as foster kids 15 years ago, immediately beat up every tough guy and started selling dope. Rupert said their real father was a Special Services officer who was killed overseas. I believed him. I once saw the Stanleys take on half-a-dozen idiots from a football team during lunch break and finish them off without a scratch.

Thankfully, however, the Stanleys weren't ones for bullying, not once they'd taken over the roost. They instead became quasi guardians among the various dope-smoking and drinking rings about the hills. People came to them with problems and, if some crew from the city came up and caused trouble, it would be the Stanleys who made sure they left in an ambulance.

Personally, I've never had much to do with them. Whenever I've tried talking to them, I've generally been drunk, and it's rare that I make friends in that state.

A triple-fanged werewolf creature leaps onto the screen and bites the Stanley's avatar. He dies and the Stanley returns to the start of the level.

'Looks like you got done there, mate.'

'Yeeep,' the Stanley replies in a slow, crackled voice.

There's a *crack* as the plastic controller bounces off my knee and lands in my lap.

'You wanna shot?' the beast says, looking at me with black eyes and a half-open cavernous mouth. His voice is like slow-motion audio: deep, elongated, strangely distorted.

'Ah, nah. Thanks, man. I'm only here for a bit, to see Rupert, wherever he's gone.'

'Have a shot.' The Stanley turns his head back to the screen, the fake leather couch creaking with the movement of his neck. He reaches out to collect a dirty water bong from the coffee table and an equally grubby looking lighter.

'Hey, man. I heard those things aren't any good for ya. Water vapour in your lungs or something.'

The Stanley regards me again and his eyes are blacker than ever. I wish I'd never said a word. He's not human. This is a demon in the disguised form of an overly large pothead.

'Have a shot.'

I inspect the controller. It has about eight different buttons in various ergonomic positions, and a mini joystick my thumb is supposed to manipulate.

'You seen Rupert?' I ask, my voice small and ineffectual.

The Stanley strikes a cigarette lighter and sucks his bong.

I edge the joystick forward and on the screen my avatar enters a ghost town alleyway. I push buttons and a large gun appears and rattles off rounds into a wall.

'Conserve your ammo,' the Stanley whines, holding in a lungful of smoke. He exhales and a majestic cloud blankets the colour spectrums of the screen.

I push on into the slum. A thing with five arms, a witch's face and decomposing legs jumps at me.

'Eeeww,' it wails.

I clatter off rounds and miss, hitting the wall instead. It breaks apart and more wretched beings enter the valley.

'Shit,' I say.

'You're getting killed,' responds the Stanley.

Assorted monsters descend upon me in a lunging ballet of zombies, blood and gore. My gun goes *click click click* because it's out of ammunition. The witch leaps forward, opens her ghastly mouth of rotting teeth and blistering tongues, and the screen goes red.

'Man,' I say. 'That was intense.'

The Stanley reaches over and takes the controller from me.

'Are there any vampires in this game?'

'I just blast the fuck out of everything,' the Stanley shrugs. He restarts the game and in five seconds kills everything that destroyed me.

'I think I'll go look for Rupert. The bastard's meant to be getting me a drink.'

'In the fridge.'

The statement stuns me for a second.

'Rupert's in the fridge?'

'There's a bottle of Bushmills. Get me one too.'

'Oh, yeah. Right.'

The armchair tries to stick to my T-shirt as I get to my feet. I enter the kitchen, which is partly separated from the lounge room by a flimsy wall partition. There are bottles, dirty plates, rotting chicken carcasses, empty spaghetti tins and wrappers covering every available space. Frying pans and saucepans fill the sink with a congealed and solidifying mixture of grease, brown water and hopeless detergent.

I look over the carnage for a vessel safe enough to drink from. All the glasses have something growing in them. I give up and pull on the fridge door. It produces a wet, tearing sound as the seals give way and I immediately see two of three things I need: one, a column of plastic, disposable cups 'chilling' on an otherwise empty shelf, and two, a bottle of expensive looking Scotch.

There's not a Coke bottle in sight.

Poking about the kitchen, I unearth a two-litre plastic bottle with half a cup of flat, sugary cola in its bottom. There's barely enough for two drinks, but maybe the Stanley doesn't want Coke.

'Hey, man. You want Coke in your Scotch?' I say, stepping from the kitchen opening.

The giant pauses his game and swivels his entire upper torso around to regard me.

'What?'

'Do you want Coke?' I say, stepping backwards in surprise.

'Coke,' he states, black eyes staring terribly into my own. The controller drops unnoticed from his hand.

I don't get it. What's he looking at me like that for? I back away towards the entrance, air ascending at my feet, my body light-weighted and aerated.

'Ah, don't worry about it,' I say with a tremor. 'The Coke's flat.'

'You pour *Coke* in that fine Irish *whiskey* and I'll pull your fucking eyes out.'

He sits poised on his couch, ready to leap.

'Oh,' I say. 'You have … *whiskey* in there. Sorry, I only found Scotch. Where's the, where's the whiskey?'

'In the *fridge*!'

'Right.'

I step quickly inside the kitchen, my skin prickling, my neck hairs tingling. But the sound of video game is yet to resume. I wonder if he's sneaking towards the kitchen, silently, an oversized ninja preparing to extract my eyes.

Fuck you, Rupert. This place is a dungeon asylum. But then it strikes me. Where is Rupert, and where's the other Stanley? Opposite the kitchen a hallway stretches away from the lounge room in damp disrepair. There are three doors set into it and one of them is shut.

'Have you got a fucking drink yet? Hurry up and get your arse down here.'

'Yeah, in a sec. Just gonna go find Rupert.'

'You don't just gotta go do anything. Stop fucking around and get a drink.'

Something starts to worm its way into my head, an idea that makes my teeth grind. I wonder how it's been kept subterranean for so long, how it's not common knowledge, how these two beasts are not loathed by the stoners who rely on them.

I take a step towards the hallway but an immense shape slips silently into my path, parting the air like it's melted cheese.

Shit. He *is* a ninja.

'Where you going?' The Stanley's voice is low and quiet. I have to look up to address his face where a wicked black grin slashes it in two.

'I, ah, gotta find Rupert,' I say.

'No you don't.'

'I don't?'

'No.'

'But we've gotta go. I've gotta get Rupert.'

'You can go, but Rupert's not ready to go.'

'Why not? What's he doing?'

The Stanley reaches a trunk-sized arm out and grabs me behind the neck. I'm not sure what's more painful, his grip, or the weight of the thing upon my shoulders. He turns my head so my body follows and I face the loungeroom where the TV has been switched over to the news.

'Go sit down.'

He propels me forward and I stumble all the way to the armchair.

'Channel 3 director Max Reaper has denied his Federal Election coverage is biased towards conservative outfit, Family Power,' a male ABC news reader says on the TV.

The Stanley re-emerges from the kitchen, holding two plastic cups. He hands me mine before sitting down. I hold the cup in my hand and prepare to shoot it.

'The Greens today accused Channel 3 of featuring Family Power in 80 per cent of its bulletins —

'Sip it!' orders the Stanley 'You don't shoot good whiskey.'

'Right,' I say.

' — but Reaper said his network was simply the victim of a witch hunt by quasi communists committed to banning free speech.'

Footsteps approach from the hallway. It's Rupert but he turns at the hallway opening and heads straight out the screen door, a bottle of Scotch in his hand.

'Rupert,' I shout.

The screen door clatters shut behind him.

I shoot the Stanley's whiskey down and slam the plastic cup upon the coffee table to get up before he can say a word. *Shoop* goes the fake leather, sticking ever more resiliently to my back.

Explosions and screams of computer violence chase me outside into the dry, bright, drought-ridden winter air.

'Rupert,' I shout. Then I see him. He's sitting in the passenger seat of Biddie's car. 'What the hell are you doing, man?'

I run down the lawn to the car.

'It's time to go, Pete,' he says softly, his sweaty face pale and depressed.

'No shit it's time to go, you moron. What the hell were you doing back there?'

'What do you fucking care?'

'What?'

'Are you driving or do you want me to?'

'I don't get it, man,' I say, climbing quickly into the driver's seat. 'Something's weird in that place. What are you hanging there for?'

We drive out of the Stanleys' front yard and into the streets of Blackwood. My tongue feels starved of saliva. I need a chaser for the Stanley's whiskey.

'Sick and tired of your backyard looking like something the dog dug up?' Biddie's car radio erupts. 'Be the envy of friends with a brand new outdoor furniture suite from Harold's Homeware.'

'I fucking hate this thing,' I say, pushing at radio buttons.

'The cops are after me,' Rupert says.

'Ah, bullshit. How'd you work that out?'

His lips tighten and he looks out the windscreen.

' ... selection of barbecues, or how about an outdoor wood oven to impress your mates with gourmet pizza?'

I hit the radio face and it changes to pop music with a tinny doof doof beat.

'Man, the cops weren't even there,' I say. 'If they knew who it was who smashed up those TVs, they would have caught you already. You spoken to your Mum? Ten bucks says they've never even called.'

'Fuck Mum.'

'Yeah, well fuck you, you nutty fuck.'

The taste of the Stanley's whiskey is changing. It's becoming warm, savoury … even pleasant.

Fucking whiskey toffs.

'What's your problem, hey?' Rupert turns to face me. 'Who the hell are you to come find me and start hassling me? And what's with all this judgement? You're a fucking drunk, that's what you are. Don't you get all high and mighty with me, Peter.'

'Don't go calling me Peter, Rupert.'

'Peter,' he says harshly.

'Shut up, man.'

'Yeeeah Adelaide!' wails a loud-mouthed disc jockey. 'Who's out to party tonight? The weather's warm and, okay so it's winter and it should be cold and wet, but, hey, it's Saturday night and —

I hit the radio angrily and it stutters between stations.

'Peter who thinks he's Mister Together. Peter who thinks he knows more about anyone than everyone. Peter who thinks 'cause his *fiancé* wants his blood he's got problems. You don't even know what problems are.'

'Shut up, Rupert. She's not my fiancé anymore.'

'Peter the fucking pisshead who's always looking for excuses to get drunk.'

'Oh, yeah, this is good coming from you.'

'Who's got anger management issues, who hates everything and everyone, who really just wants to sit down and cry.'

The skin beneath my fingernails burns with rage.

'At least I'm not stupid enough to be sucking arse with the Stanleys just 'cause I'm a paranoid twat.'

'I ain't no fucking twat.'

We approach the main road of Blackwood. I push the accelerator and the back end of Biddie's car swings out as we turn towards Belair. A couple of teenagers in hoodies raise their arms in approval from the footpath.

'You bloody well look like one right now, you little ponce. They tears in your eyes?'

'Piss off.'

Biddie's automatic transmission shifts steadily into high gear. The speedometer rises towards 80.

'How's your butt feeling, slave?'

'What?'

'Does is hurt to sit down? Do you like the Stanleys' cock up your arse?'

'I'm gonna fucking hit you.'

I swing the car into the opposite lane to overtake a ute before swinging back in front of it. They flash their headlights but in a matter of seconds they're car lengths behind.

'Or maybe that ain't your thing. Maybe you only like to suck. Tell me, Rupert, does it taste like fine Irish *whiskey*?'

Rupert's fist crashes into my upper arm. It hurts, but I can't think about the pain because his assault has caused me to swing the car into the opposite lane again where a Mitsubishi all-wheel-drive is head-on about 10 metres.

'Good one, Rupert!'

I lurch the wheel back to the left. Biddie's rear end swings about with a squeal of wheels but lingers in the oncoming lane.

'Man, you're weird,' Rupert says.

The Mitsubishi collides into our rear panel. *Crunch*, metal upon metal — the noise of a Transformer hawking up a loogie. The impact sends us careering but I manage to maintain some control as our car slows, my left foot heavy on the brakes while the other remains flat on the accelerator.

Fuck, I hate the sound of metal.

'Yeah? Well what else were you doing back there?'

Now the ute we overtook seconds ago rams straight into our rear end, shoving us forward so our heads whip forward and back, pushing the car's speed up again, my left foot abandoning the brake.

'Yeah, 'cause that's what I was doing, Pete. I was back there sucking cock. You're a weird mother —

The ute driver fires his horn, drowning out the rest of Rupert's insult. I look in my rear-view mirror and see our rear bumper is caught in the ute's front bumper and we're dragging it along, or it's pushing us along, one of the two.

'Hang on.'

I yank the steering wheel to the right, drawing squeals from the ute's wheels. I rip it back to the left. Metal groans and engines wail but still the ute is attached and still its horn blasts into the cabin.

In the rear-view mirror I see a bald, stocky-looking driver with a leather-tan face shouting from the panel van, waving his arms frantically. I wave back.

'You think I'm fucking the Stanleys?' Rupert bleats, oblivious to the road carnage we're entangled in. 'Is that what you think? Seriously? Who's the crazy bastard —

The ute's front bumper finally disengages, creating a metallic ripping sound that tears through my bones.

'I fucking hate the sound of metal!' I scream.

Biddie's engine hollers red while its wheels struggle for purchase. I push the accelerator flat to the floor.

'You're a fucking nutcase, Pete.'

'Well, what else were you doing? I saw the shut door. I saw your sick looking face. You were supposed to get me a fucking drink, not sucking off some bald psycho.'

'Shut up!'

Beneath the chaos a banging sound emerges from the back of the car.

'Great. And now we've gone and fucked up Biddie's car.'

'Well, maybe you ought to learn to drive.'

Rupert attacks me again, this time punching my thigh.

'Good one, dickhead,' I shout as my other leg reacts by shooting upwards to squash into the steering wheel, turning the car now travelling at 90kph towards the shoulder of the road.

'Shit.'

Banging in the boot. A muffled voice yelling.

'And what the hell *is* that?' Rupert shouts, cocking his thumb to the back of the car, ignoring the fact we're hurtling towards a paint shop.

'That's what I've been trying to say. I've got a problem!'

The front of Biddie's car lifts into the air as it hits the footpath. I turn the steering wheel to the right but it doesn't matter. The front wheels aren't even on the ground.

Crunch.

We land on top of a signpost and bend it to the ground. The rear end swings out again, this time to the left. Primary colours splatter over Rupert's side of the car as we take out a dozen cans of paint on the footpath display.

'Bloody hell.'

But we're still moving along the footpath, the sign post banging and clattering against components of machinery beneath. I glance at the road to our side. All the cars have stopped, waiting for our deadly circus to end.

'Get me the hell out of here,' the fake Jesus screams.

'Who's in there?' Rupert asks, looking back at the boot.

I focus on getting Biddie's car back onto the road. We plonk off the footpath and there's a screeching sound as some section of Biddie's car drags along the tarmac and falls of. I accelerate.

'It doesn't matter right now, slave. We've gotta get off the main road.'

'Fuck you,' Rupert shouts into my ear, before opening the door like he's about to jump out.

'Shut the door. You're getting paint inside.'

'You crazy fools, let me out of this car!'

'Shut up,' Rupert and I say in unison.

Rupert slams his door shut but, to my dismay, its shock on the beaten car causes the boot latch to click open. Biddie's now horribly smashed and dented boot flips open in my rear view mirror.

'You're an arsehole, Peter.'

'Stop saying my name like that.'

A turn-off to the left is approaching. It will take us to a winding series of mountain bike tracks that descend the scrub-covered hills to the flats, well away from the carnage we've caused.

'Peter Peter Peter.'

'Slave boy fucking lapdog.'

Rupert screams. He launches upon me and starts hitting my arms and legs.

The stink of his three-day binge is catastrophic.

I tug the wheel around to the left and speed down the road at 80kph.

'Do you wanna fucking crash?'

'Aghhh,' Rupert hollers, landing a solid punch to my shoulder that deadens it immediately.

'Stop it, man. I can't see. Jesus is in the boot.'

'Aghhh,' he continues, hitting me in the face, and I'm always so shocked by that first blow. It's so rude, so utterly confronting, sharp and incendiary.

Gritting my teeth into hammered steel, I take my hands off the wheel, grab Rupert by the skull, and shove him away so his head hits the passenger window.

I'm about to punch him when the rocky face of a hill launches before us.

'Shit!'

We thump into the hill and dirt falls onto the bonnet, onto the windscreen. Our bodies leap out of our seats and smash into the dashboard, the steering wheel, the glove box. The neck of Rupert's Scotch is knocked off and amber flows onto his shoes, the floor mat, the carpet. The car motor chokes horribly and stops firing, flooded, exhausted.

We sit in silence for a moment as hot metal ticks from the engine bay.

Rupert comes back to life first. He reaches down to his feet and rights the jagged bottle of Scotch before sitting back in his seat, nursing a wound on his cheek that sprouts a thin band of blood. I poke over my ribs to see if anything's broken. Knife-edge beams of sunlight slice the air, igniting dust particles, dirt and all ever else thrown into the air to descend silently about us like snow.

It's peaceful — until Biddie's car radio inexplicably erupts into life.

'Need a new suit?' asks a shouting man. 'How about a pair of shoes to match? Buy any outfit at Ronnies and we'll also throw in a tie, cufflinks and belt. Buy in the next 48 hours and we'll even throw in a beard trimmer because, let's face it, it might be hot out there but you've gotta look smoking.'

Rupert leans forward and softly touches the correct button to silence the radio. He looks exhausted.

'What *were* you doing back there then?' I say.

'He makes me … ' Rupert sighs defeatedly and closes his eyes. 'He makes me dress his feet. He has severe athlete's foot and can't handle the sight of it.'

I imagine Rupert kneeling in front of the Stanley and attending to his feet, the bald-headed monster sitting back in a chair, averting his eyes.

'*That's* what you do?'

'Twice a day.'

'That's it?'

'That's it, then I can hang around as much as I like.'

I digest the ridiculous information, yet I can see Rupert is telling the truth. He looks utterly ashamed.

'Why … why can't the other Stanley do it?'

Rupert fingers at the broken neck of his Scotch bottle.

'I have to do his feet too. It grosses them both out.'

I start laughing. It develops quickly from tiny, machine gun spurts of air, into a full blown, croaky mess.

A twinkle returns to Rupert's eyes and he starts laughing too — a high-pitched, golden tinkle of beauty. It's utterly infectious and reminds me of happier days. I laugh harder, tears in my eyes. Rupert begins to salivate, spittle running down his chin. We re-unite as haggard friends from a generation of brats who lost their shit too young.

There's a thud from the back of Biddie's car and it rocks on what's left of the suspension. The open boot wobbles and we can hear feet running away.

'Shit.'

I open the door and leap out the car. Rupert follows, or tries to. His door has become jammed in the collision.

'Get him, Pete,' he shouts.

There's no time to answer. A billowing white frock and flowing brown hair is running up the road.

I give chase.

3:15pm

To my right are steep driveways, houses on stilts. To my left is scrub, a gully of walking trails that continue downwards to the suburbs two kilometres away. Ahead of me is a man dressed as Jesus with bruises on his face.

I run after him, warm air pushing at my hair, at my clothes, a pursuit through open space that should have been invigorating if it wasn't so hot. Dry oxygen scratches at the lining of my throat. The fake Jesus pulls away from me up the scorching asphalt and I push my legs faster, matching his pace, but I can't gain ground. He risks a quick glance back at me, his sandals pounding the road, eyes wide-open and desperate.

'Oi,' I shout.

He stumbles and lifts his hand to his ear, clawing frantically like something's fallen out. While he's still moving forward, he twists to look at the ground behind him, his sandals sliding over loose gravel as he leans backwards to retrieve whatever he's dropped. The gap between us closes as the fake Jesus grabs his property, looking up at me in fear, before turning around to begin running again. But I have the momentum.

'No,' he cries.

'Oompf,' I reply as I crash into him and we fall to the road.

My knees and my right elbow scrape along the asphalt. His back and his arse do the same under the extra weight of my own. Limbs flap and flail as we stop; ribs twist and contort. I struggle and squeeze, gaining purchase on both his wrists and pushing them to the ground. His legs continue to thrash and kick, now kneeing me in the inner thigh, now kicking me in the ankle.

'Hold still.'

'Leave me alone.'

'Shut up,' I hiss. I try to place a hand over his mouth, continuing to hold down his arms with my elbows.

One of them breaks free and rips at my hair.

'Aghhh,' I cry, reaching up to prise his grip away.

His other hand scratches my cheek.

I want to punch him, but I have to get his hand out of my hair. The pain is unbearable.

'Rupert,' I scream.

'Yes?' He says, panting, standing over us.

'Don't just stand there.'

The fake Jesus knees me in the coccyx.

'Ow. Do something!'

'Why's this guy dressed like Jesus?'

The gnawing, growling animal beneath me continues to pull my hair.

'Rupert, if you don't fucking well … oompf … get this bastard away from me … I'm gonna … '

Rupert manoeuvres above the man's head, reaches down and grabs him beneath both arms.

'Noooo,' the robed bastard wails, kicking and spitting yet still gripping my hair.

I manage to whip out a fist and punch him in the stomach. It's soft like a sponge. He lets go of my hair and collapses onto the ground coughing.

Rupert pulls the fake Jesus upright and looks over his shoulder at me with sparkling eyes.

'What's going on, Pete?'

'We've … we've gotta get him back to the car and get out of here.' I get to my knees and try and catch my breath.

'Who is he?'

The row of houses tower over the road to our right. I can feel their occupants staring from between drawn curtains. No doubt the cops have already been called.

'We've gotta get out of here. I'll explain in the car.'

'You kidnap this guy?' Rupert says, starting to vibrate on the spot.

'Rupert, let's move.'

'Wow, man.' He pushes the now thoroughly dejected looking fake Jesus back down the road. 'I thought you were just talking about Leanne. I thought she'd just done something new, like, I don't know, fucking cut off your balls while you were sleeping. I didn't think you were doing anything like this. This is wild, man. This is crazy. What'd he do?'

'Just move. If he shouts or anything, hit him.'

Biddie's car comes into view as we round a bend. The rear end is completely smashed in and the bumper's gone. It's a wonder I didn't crush the fake Jesus to death in that boot. The rear side panel that hit the Mitsubishi is a crumpled piece of cardboard, streaked with blue from the other car's paint.

'Oh, crap.'

'Wait till you see the other side.'

I move over to the road's edge and step backwards in surprise. The whole left side is a Pro Hart mural of abstract shapes, colours, and dripping paint that streaks from the side of the white bonnet all the way to the left rear wheel. Amazingly, the bonnet isn't buckled in. The face of the hill was more loose soil than rocks. With any luck, the engine might start.

'Pretty cool, huh?'

'Put him in the car, man.'

'I think you'd better tell me what's going —

'Just do it.'

Rupert opens a psychedelic door and pushes the fake Jesus onto the back seat, leaving a red handprint on the back of his frock. A quick but violent arrow of guilt pierces my chest.

Scarlet upon white — I hate that mix.

It mixes with Leanne's face and breaks my heart. But then I notice a flesh-coloured wire poking out of the fake Jesus' fist. I lean into the car to try and take it but he pulls away. I grab his wrist and squeeze with all my strength, sinews recoiling under my touch, until he finally relents.

'Damn you, ' the fake Jesus hisses as his precious cargo falls onto the seat. It's a skin-coloured wire connected to a transparent earpiece. It looks modern, professional and dangerous.

Dread plunges into my stomach.

'Rupert, we've gotta get out of here, man,' I say, picking the earpiece up and throwing it quickly outside where I crush it with my foot. 'We've gotta get out of here right now.'

But Rupert's face is white as he stares at the ruined device. His body is taut. He chews like a horse, spitting, dripping, wiping his mouth with the back of his hand, staring at me wide-eyed, horrified, amphetamised. He begins stepping in tiny movements towards the front of the car, a dedicated robot on failing batteries.

'What … what did you get me into?' he stammers through gnashing teeth.

'*C'mon* man. I'll tell you in the car.'

I climb into the driver's seat and turn the ignition. Biddie's starter motor whines reluctantly for a moment until the engine kicks over with a clatter. I slam the transmission into reverse, one foot on the brake to pause for my petrified friend. But Rupert's not getting into the car. He's at the door, shaking, various colours of paint smeared over his clothes.

'C'mon man –

'Shut up,' he says. 'Just shut up. I didn't want this. I didn't want any of this. I don't know what you're doing, man. I just wanna be at the Stanleys. You shouldn't have come here, man. You shouldn't have come at all.'

'Shit.' I put it in neutral and stand out of the car to look over the roof at Rupert. 'Look, man. This guy walked in off the beach today, out of nowhere, saying he's Jesus. But he's not. He's a fake. The whole thing was staged. I don't know how, but just look at him.'

The fraud looks at me hatefully through the window.

'See what I mean? But the cops are gonna be here any minute, and with all that paint over the car, we stand out like dogs balls.'

'You shouldn't have come, man,' Rupert mumbles as he climbs rigidly into the car, his face the colour of leafless trees in dark winters from faraway places on TV.

I reverse out of the dent we've put into the hill and we rattle down the road, turning onto a fire track that will take us into scrubland.

Rupert lifts his jagged bottle and pours Scotch down his throat.

"The following rant was left for me by Peter Mackay on our dining room table approximately two weeks before separation." LT

I would like to say sorry but I'm not. There's nothing friendly about RADIOS any more. This City of Information has LOST THE PLOT. All these radio ads, TV ads, YouTube ads, internet pop-ups and BLOATED WHALE advertising, it never stops. Everywhere you look somebody's trying to need you something, buy you something, EAT YOU SOMETHING. They even have ads at the cinema. They're ten foot tall, go for half an hour in surround sound and THERE IS NO ESCAPE.

I must be different. Adverts don't make me want to buy something. They make me want to HIT something. Every time a dickhead with white teeth bites into a hamburger, every time some urban COOK with modern hair tells me about his dead SQUID, I want to stretch it over his face and suffocate him, and don't even TALK about families in urban four-wheel-drives. That shit makes me want to drop ATOMIC BOMBS. It's like sinking your face into a blowhole, a salesperson pit, mad MIDGETS from Wonka's sucker factory saturating you with rotting spermaceti. It freaks me out, shits me, terrorises me, makes me WANT TO SCREAM. And the noise, the fucking ADVERTS tearing at my head, bashing at my skull, outfits, hairdos, whitegoods, furniture warehouses, fucking reality shows. It turns my body inside out, cuts my kidneys with plastic, swipes bank cards across my lungs. It's not normal. It's not life. Please tell me, Leanne, please. How can all these people live in this filth and let it become the soundtrack to their lives?

Yes, I smashed your radio, but don't blame me. The adverts made me do it.

SUNDAY

I'm standing in a room of beautiful women. They wear tight outfits that leave little to the imagination. They wear jeans; they wear short skirts; they wear black dresses and black singlets. They stand around talking to each other, their faces bathed in colours from widescreen TVs that cover the walls with fast food advertising, news reports and modern vampire movies. Every now and then they flash their teeth at me. Long and sharp, their teeth are the same. All are white. All their fangs point perfectly downwards.

I want to move but I can't. I want to embrace each of them in turn, a spider enclosing a nest of bugs, but my body is paralysed. It's bound by unseen forces.

Their leader, the head vampress, steps in front of them with one hand behind her back. She looks at my crotch.

I realise I'm naked and my desire's in full view.

C'mon, I want to say. Get it over with. But all I can manage is garbles and stifled grunts from lips that won't move.

She bares her teeth. Hers are wet with green, oozing goo, and her flock is getting restless. They hiss and claw at their pillows, glaring at me suggestively. Their leader edges closer. She steps backwards and lifts what she holds behind her back into view.

It's a head, the head of the Old Man. His rotted face glares at me with hate.

'Wake the fuck up, Peter,' says the decapitated head.

It sounds like Biddie's voice.

'You're making me sick. Wake *up*!'

It's dark. The vampires are gone. I'm sitting down and can't move. Somebody's breathing nearby.

'Biddie?' I try to say, but there's something woolly stuffed in my mouth. About me are shadows and tiny echoes of my efforts from walls that are close. The room spins, rotating on a 45-degree angle. Dim outlines of shadows and walls slide diagonally past my vision in nauseating, repetitive motion.

My arms are stuck behind my back where something clasps them together. My legs can't move either. In my shorts, my other limb is shifty and agitated. The rest of my body aches with the familiar decay of a hangover.

'You happy now?' says Biddie's voice at the same time as my fragmented mind produces another image of the Old Man's decapitated head.

'What the fuck?' I attempt to say but nothing more than a muffled gloop comes out my mouth. Fabric fills my mouth, and against the back of my throat, where it's dry, where it's dehydrated, where the little uvula hangs by a thread, the wool prickles my flesh and makes me cough.

'Calm down before you suffocate,' says the reappearing head.

'Stop it,' I choke. My expanding ribs feel like they're breaking apart.

'Don't try to talk. It only makes it worse.' The head disappears but Biddie's voice is unmistakable.

'You need to take a good look at yourself.' Now it's Leanne's voice in the darkness, her stern tone, her serious concern for the man she intends to marry. 'Drinking is not the answer.'

Bile seeps into my mouth against the wool. Bile comes out my tear ducts. Bile leaks out my ears and drips onto my shoulders. It's acid and will eat into my clothes, my skin, my ribcage, and finally my gut from where it came and cause me to shit myself. The shit will be hot. It will ruin my pants, burn a hole in my seat, cause me to collapse while my arms remain tied so my backbone snaps. All that remains will be skin and sinews.

My torso convulses and vomit pours into my mouth. My breastplate cracks with pain and fear seizes my brain — I can't breathe.

Panic.

Contractions rack my body. Splotches of bright lights flash in my vision as my nostrils suck desperately for air. I manage to swallow and dirty warmth retreats down my oesophagus. A few more swallows and there's space for oxygen. I shut my eyes tight and try to ignore the spinning.

'Oh, Peter. You're such a dramatist.'

Shut up, cow.

Never said that to her at the time. I just wanted to get away from her, from her caring mind, her loving eyes, her simplistic view of life and her belief in it.

I want her now.

'Shit, Peter,' says Biddie. 'Vomit? There's no air in here as it is.'

I open my eyes. The room has slowed its spin. Vomit is good for that, even if you do have to swallow it. I blink hard against the tears and look at the shadows surrounding me.

The biggest one is in front of me.

'Biddie?' I ask with a muffled voice.

'I thought Rupert was the crazy bastard who got us all in trouble. What the hell were you thinking?'

'What's going on?'

'You stupid drunk bastard.'

'Are we dead?'

'You're gonna be, once we get out of here, dickhead.'

'Whatever,' I say, but the shadow of Biddie continues to lay into me.

'Not only did you leave me on the beach, smash up my car and get me involved with whatever fucking mess you're in, but I've gotta sit here, tied up in a fucking shed, and listen to you moan and groan like you're having some kind of sick wet dream. You fucking prick.'

Bloody Rupert and his Scotch.

Flash in my mind to our interrogation in the scrub, how we parked the car and tied the fake Jesus to the tow bar with octopus straps and paced about, how we started seriously — or I started seriously — asking questions, demanding answers, all the time drinking from the broken bottle neck of the Scotch, drinking it straight, swigging it down, walking to the side of the clearing from time to time to piss into the scrub.

I wanted to hit him again but I didn't.

Flash in my mind to the onset of drunkenness, the onset of dim-wittedness, the seriousness of the situation falling into a haze of alcohol and stupid fun we embraced all too eagerly after a stressful day.

Dammit, I wish I could find some control.

Flash in my mind to Rupert's cheerful face as he danced about the fake Jesus, recording him with Biddie's video camera, asking him to dance, asking him to do magic, singing Christmas carols and touching the imposter's long brown hair, the sun setting over distant suburbs, Biddie's car covered in paint and the obscenities we drew in it for fun.

Shit.

Flash in my mind to the fake Jesus saying he was an actor, how I said I knew it from the start, how he revealed he likes doing plays the most. He even became proud when he told us of a play he was in at the Sydney Opera House.

I said all actors are fakes. He went silent after that.

Flash in my mind to our indifference. Of the fact that we had run out of booze and needed more. Of the fact it was dark and we should be able to get away with driving again. We drove illegally on mountain bike trails to the flats, to suburbia that stretched nearly 10 kilometres to the city, to a bottle shop in Mitcham, parking out back while Rupert went in. I went to a phone and called Biddie.

He wasn't happy.

Flash in my mind to Rupert and me giggling as Biddie screamed down the line, calling me an arsehole, calling me a wanker, threatening to club me.

Flash in my mind to how we drove back up the hill to Biddie's house where we beeped the horn over and over, how Biddie came roaring out his front door, how he ripped open my door before he stopped and looked at his car, at the dents, circling it to see the paint, the boot, Rupert's laughing face guzzling beer in the back with the fake Jesus sitting silent, refusing to have the beer that Rupert offered him every couple of minutes or so.

And then, then there was confusion, black vans screeching up, people moving fast, large thugs pouring out of the vans. Somebody pulled me from our car and threw me to another guy who threw me to another.

Flash in my mind to Biddie fighting, of him punching someone and holding them off before another guy tackled him, all of them in black, all of them large, all of them fast and professional, like ex-FBI gangsters from American movies, and Rupert's screaming, Rupert's wailing, somebody's holding me telling the others to go and grab Rupert, five shapes holding a thrashing, howling monkey on speed who scratched, flailed, bit and kicked, punched and twisted in the air to fall down, get up again, run into somebody's front yard and down the side of their house, all the time shouting, all the time hollering, the thugs freaking out, giving up the chase and running back to shove me in a van, the fake Jesus getting into another van, street lights shining on the scene with an end-of-the-world orange glow.

I started shouting, until somebody shoved a sock in my mouth, thudded the back of my head and then … and then …

Now I'm in darkness. I'm still drunk but feel hungover at the same time. The room stinks of vomit and my friend in the darkness is angry with me. He wants to kill me. I can feel it. The urge is pouring into the room with every expulsion of his dark, shadowy breath.

'Sorry, man.'

'Spit the sock out of your mouth,' Biddie says. 'I can't understand a fucking word you say.'

The problem with Biddie is he's smug. His arms might be tied behind his back and his legs to a chair base, but his face remains calm and composed, fixed with an 'I-told-you-so' smirk from beneath the black sunglasses he somehow managed to keep wearing. His expression hasn't changed since dawn poked through the rust holes of our otherwise empty shed two hours ago.

My eyes crawl about the small space for things to look at — the walls, the floor, the sunlight beaming through the dusty air, anything but the smirk in front of me. But when I give up and close my eyes, I feel it upon my face, dismantling my features, my personality, my virtues and failings, observing my insecurity, the little bits of dried vomit plastered upon my chin.

It was better when it was dark. It was better when Biddie was just a presence, a voice, a second party to the long discussion that we managed throughout the hours of darkness.

It was a good discussion. It was an in-depth discussion. Everything was my fault, of course. I should never have been involved, but we did manage to theorise on what this was about, who these Jesus people might be, how they got those fish to surge, how they made the beach scene appear suitably unearthly.

The motives behind the hoax were my own ideas: its organisers meant for the waking world to lap it up, to believe that Jesus had returned and it was time to start behaving. It was all about control.

Biddie called me a fool.

I called him a wanker.

Biddie said he went straight home after I fled the beach. He had to catch a taxi and already people were talking. Something had happened. Something paranormal had begun. Finally, in our desperate age of obscene consumption, something had arrived to reassure us we were on the right path.

When Biddie arrived home he saw the beach on his TV, the Second Coming televised via a dozen smartphone videos. They recorded Jesus walking down the jetty, actors falling to their knees, Jesus disappearing into the dunes with a reassuring wave. The news anchor said he'd vanished just as he had appeared, back into thin air.

Biddie didn't know that I'd kidnapped the fake Jesus. He thought I'd just freaked out and left. He said I was acting more and more crazy these days. Nothing surprised him anymore.

'You know what else was crazy?' Biddie said. 'They had better footage taken from a boat. They said an amateur filmmaker caught Jesus by chance, but it wasn't amateur. It was bloody professional looking.'

He said police were making statements on the news, saying the events were unclear and people shouldn't jump to conclusions. A politician called a press conference, some guy from the Family Power Party. He called on society to 'embrace the Lord for He has come to guide us from darkness'.

There was more footage from the beach, people arriving in droves. All over the city, people were talking about something that had only happened two hours ago and buying the hoax in blind hope.

'Somebody's spreading the news,' I said. 'Somebody had the media prepared.'

'Man, you really are starting to sound more and more like Rupert,' Biddie replied.

'Whoever was in the boat must have seen me,' I continued. 'They must have seen that I was your friend. They must have followed you home and waited for me to turn up.'

Biddie didn't say anything, but I could see he was angry.

'Well, they weren't following *me*,' I said. 'I was acting smart.'

'You recruited Rupert. Can't be that smart.'

'Fuck off.'

Biddie laughed.

'When we get out of here,' I said, 'we should see this thing to the end, expose the hoax.'

'You already had that chance.'

'Well somebody has to do it. Somebody has to grind the coffee and shove it up the pigs' arses.'

'What's the difference?' Biddie said, his trademark response to anything that looked challenging.

That was last night. Now the sun has risen. The booze has worn off. I have a dry mouth and palpitating heart.

No alcohol.

It's a foreign situation, not for the fact we've been kidnapped, but because we have to spend so much time in a room together without anything to distract our attention, like alcohol. Friends ought to have something to say to each other when they're not drunk, or at the least be secure in each other's company. We've none of this. There's only self-righteous Biddie sitting in front of me, watching, timing to see how long it takes for me to break, for me to start crying, for me to start screaming out to our captors and beg for release.

The thought had occurred to me.

But Biddie doesn't understand my anger — I stole the fake Jesus without thinking about it. My interrogation in the scrub — it was good and achieved something out of the chaos, until I became drunk, until I became useless and dimwitted, until I stupidly drove to Biddie's house when we should have taken the fake Jesus straight to the media.

Now I'm tied to a chair in a little shed that's growing hot. The sun's only been up two hours and I'm already starting to sweat — and it's meant to be winter.

I need Rupert, Rupert with his manic freakdom yet easily pliable loyalty, Rupert with his twinkling smile, a nature that never intends to put people at unease but does so anyway because he's fucking mad. He would encourage me to make a stand. He would act crazy, nuts, and just being around him in his natural state would make me feel less crazy and nuts, not because I'm stable, but because compared to him I am as steady as a rock.

What's the difference? What's the difference?

'Man, I'm starting to get thirsty,' I say.

Biddie doesn't answer.

Prick.

'Shit, man. Is this drought ever gonna break?'

What's the difference? What's the difference?

'When these guys come back,' I continue, 'we should jump them as soon as they set us free. Or actually, maybe we should wait a bit to see how many there are.'

'What makes you think they're gonna set us free?'

Finally, he speaks.

'If this is some huge conspiracy like you think it is, then you and I are a real problem. So is Rupert. They're probably out there right now hunting him down.'

'You think so?' I say in an encouraging tone, willing him to keep talking. His smug silence is unbearable.

'What do you fucking think? Of course they are. Why in the hell you decided to get him involved, I'll never understand. Or me. You think this is some great fucking cause for you and your sad-sack life? What you've done, *Peter*, is probably gotten us killed.'

'Don't say my name like that.'

Biddie shakes his head and looks off to the side.

Bastard.

But he's right, of course, and suddenly I don't feel so hot anymore. Suddenly my dry mouth doesn't matter. There's been no sounds of anything outside all night. For all we know we're in the city's north, on plains renowned for murder, stuffed in a tin shed where our bodies will never be found.

'Starting to get it now, are we?'

'Shouldn't have gotten so drunk,' I murmur. 'Had it together for a while then. I had it, but … How professional did that boat footage really look?'

'About as professional as those black vans, those big bastards, and the way they've tied us up in this shit-stinking shed with no food, no water, and no chance for escape. Seriously, Peter, what in the hell were you thinking?'

'I … I was drunk when I took him, you know that, still pissed from the night before and then from your beer. But it just seemed so wrong, man. I didn't think —

'You never do. You never think of anything that matters. Only crap.'

'You don't know that.'

'Only difference between Rupert and you is that Rupert doesn't deny it.'

'You're a mean bastard, Biddie.'

'No, Peter, I just know what's what, and I don't let the shit send me sideways.'

'Don't say my name like that.'

'And why the hell not?' he snorts. 'It's your name. Is there a problem with your own name now?'

'No.' I want to get angry. I'm not prepared for this.

'Then why, Peter? C'mon, we're gonna die here. Why can't I say your name?'

''Cause —

'Peter.'

'Shut up.'

'Peter.' And still he snorts.

'I'm warning you.'

'And what are you gonna do? Break out of your chains? We're stuck, Peter. We're fucked, Peter. We're dead meat, Peter. What's the difference?'

What's the difference? What's the difference? What's the difference?

'Just —

'You know what?' he says. 'I'll tell you why.'

'Don't —

'With all your ramblings and whinging fucking rants about everything and everyone that we've all gotta hear about every fucking day of our lives, what you really can't stand is *yourself*. Isn't that right, Peter? And I don't blame you either. Fuck, I'm so sick of your face —

'No, it's not. It's because you sound like Leanne when you say my name like that.'

'Oh,' Biddie says conclusively. 'Well, there you go.'

He pauses but I know it's coming. Now he's gonna let loose. Now he's gonna show exactly why he never gets deep. The smart, smug, self-righteous son-of-a-bitch who knows me inside out, now he's gonna let me have it.

I want to shit.

'You really fucked that up, didn't you?' he says.

'Don't say it.'

'We're gonna die out here. We're gonna starve to death or die of thirst. They say it's the thirst that gets you and that means you're gonna go first. You're the one who's already dehydrated as fuck from being so pissed last night. I'm gonna be stuck sitting here looking at your dead body and smelling your shit. What's the fucking difference?'

'Take off your sunglasses,' I say feebly.

'What?'

'You think you're all stable and ... and ... and secure and better than all of us, but you can't even look me in the eye. You can't look anyone in the eye. You've always gotta have yours covered with those fucking sunglasses. No one ever knows where you're looking. Take them off.'

'What's the difference?'

What's the difference? What's the difference? What's the difference?

'Do you realise how stupid you sound when you say that?' I say.

'What's the difference?'

'What?'

'It doesn't matter what you think. You're about to die. And for the record, my hands are tied like yours, so I can't take off my sunglasses, even if I wanted to. Why did you leave Leanne?'

'What's the difference!?'

'We've gotta hear about her all the time. You're always bringing it up. But she was as good as it was ever gonna get for you. She was better than anything any of us were ever gonna score. I can't believe you pissed that away.'

'She's a difficult bitch and when I get out of here I'm gonna fight her in court.'

'We're not getting out of here. And anyway, your Nan left that house to you both. You were gonna get married. It's in the will. You don't have a case. Why'd you leave her?'

'I need a drink.'

'You drink too much.'

'Of water, you arsehole. And so do you!'

'Yeah, but I keep it under control. If I got as nutty as you I would never touch a drop.'

'Then why do you hang around, hey? Why do you keep ringing me if I'm so fucking nutty, hey? Why? I'll tell *you* why. It's because your aerated head feels big when you hang around losers like me and Rupert, doesn't it? You smug fuck.'

'Are you gonna cry now, little boy?'

'And shut up about Leanne. You don't know a damn thing.'

'Is that so, is it, Peter?'

I ignore him, wishing he went quiet again — anything but the knives launching from his mouth.

'She used to ring me, you know.'

'What?' An artery cracks black in my heart.

'All the time. When you first kicked her out. She used to ring me at work, to try and understand what the fuck was going on in your head.'

'I ... '

But I can't say anything. I feel utterly betrayed, utterly exposed, utterly naked, my deepest darkest secrets, my deepest darkest actions, my deepest darkest darkness talked about like it's gossip — to Biddie of all fucking people. Mr Stable. Mr Better-Than-You. Mr Fucking-Never-Reveal-A-Thing-About-Myself-But-I'll-Smirk-You-To-Death.

'You motherfucker.'

And Leanne! That horror, that all-deceiving, all-back-stabbing, two-faced fucking mole. I bet she told him about my 'issues'. I bet she told him about the time I cried, the time I broke down, the time I crawled up into her pillows and sobbed like a fucking little baby. I bet she told him about the fact I think everyone is dead and I hate this city and the fact I'm stuck here with every other futureless bastard and that I loathe my life. I loathe the fact I'm never gonna do a damned thing of worth. We're all just carbon-oozing, heat-inducing cogs and the wheels don't care who make up the circle, what they think, what they're good at, just as long as they do it and the job gets done and the cogs keeps turning and shut-up, boy, stop complaining, you're one of the luckiest sons of bitches in the world from the moment you were born into this great fucking country.

I bet she told him about the time we experimented in bed.

I shout. I holler. In the closed tin shed it's deafening and horrible but Biddie doesn't flinch.

I bet she told him about what I said after my Nan died, how I was more glad than sad because Nan was in so much pain, how I told Leanne in a show of bravado that I was 'thankful it happened 'cause if it took any longer I might have done it myself'. I bet she didn't tell him what happened next, how I told Leanne I was just being tough and didn't mean it, how I had to backtrack in that pathetic moment when she looked shocked, when little tiny tears welled up in her confused green eyes, the loser, the slave to emotions and idealistic luvvie fucking duvvie, an everyday computer in the form of a human head with predictable beliefs, predictable hormone patterns, predictable reactions, declarations, pledges and expectations. Because everyone's the same. Once you're past those few weeks of working each other out. Once you're past those few weeks of courtship and getting to know each other, yearning to get it on but taking it slow because you're truly interested, once you're past all the movies, the text messages at work, the keeping tabs on your new partner and the sex that starts slowly with a night or two of fooling around and getting comfortable with each other's skin, blood, wet stuff and squishy bits, once you get past the next few months of thankful lust with a partner plucked from humanity, then they look at you and there is the need, not the sexual, not the pleasurable, but the need. You are their life. You are their very motive for continuing. You are their fathers, their mothers, their idols, their hope, their future, and they don't look at you like you are you anymore. They look at you like you're *their* property, *their* very fucking life. You're a walking talking extension of *their* own appendages and you have to do all the right things because if you don't, if you make a scene, if you try to maintain your sovereignty, those little green eyes well up, those little cheeks puff out, those little wrinkles of defiance come into being and then there's an argument. Then there's a fight. There are tears. There are words spoken. There's the make-up. There's the get back together, all warm, wet, salty and nice and you have to stay at home on a Friday night, your body yearning to be out screaming and smashing glass bottles and drinking piss, mashing it up with all the other fucking faces on the weekend binge to a hell that nobody believes exists. You have to lie in bed with a sleeping fixture of fragile beauty, listen to her breathe, listen to her murmur, feel her soft arm over your neck and there's no escape. There's no end. You cannot sleep. You pull her arm away, put on your clothes and out you go. When you return, she's not asleep. She's up and she's asking questions but you're drunk, you want sex, that's all there is. You're asleep after that. That's the first time. From there it happens again and again. She cries more and more. The make-ups become more and more frequent. The cycle spins on and then she's talking of marriage when all you want to do is get the fucking hell away from her, the china, the silent nights awake while she sleeps, the fucking kitchen accessories, the garden and the back fucking yard, the fucking garage sales and auction houses on Saturdays, the buying and discussing of things you need to make your house more and more homely and peachy, and it's all upon you. *She's* upon you, looking with trust, looking with expectation, looking with love and *need*, approaching with pursed lips to perform a quick little peck like she does three times a day and sometimes you imagine accidentally pushing her off a cliff, accidentally covering her face with a cushion, accidentally squashing her head between the covers of a gigantic book so it goes snap with the intensity of a firecracker let off in an empty lounge room at midnight. The dust would rise. Dust would accost your nose. The closed pages of a relationship that delivered everything you ever dreamed you wanted since you were a little kid believing in marriage, two kids, true love and happiness would be over, done and dusted and you would have escaped. You would have made it out before it was too late. You would have given the whole disastrous affair the slip and now you have a chance to continue your life, rebuild your life, have a life and feel like you're alive once again.

I wail.

Biddie doesn't move a muscle.

In the closed tin shed it is loud, deafening, jarring and horrible 'Get me the fuck out of here!'

But you don't expect her to come back. Crying, hopeful, ever fucking hopeful like you are her own unique and definitive destiny. You don't expect her to perform her moments of womanly strength and open the door to hear her say with a carefully constructed facial expression portraying womanly resilience, 'I thought to myself, no, this can't be. You're just going through something, and I respect that, I truly do, and I want to be there for you however you want me to. Whether with you or not, it doesn't matter. I care for you deeply and truly and I won't let you go through this alone.' And it's been a couple of weeks so you let her in. You have sex, and before you know it you're back together again. And …

'Fuuuuuuuuuccckkkk.'

'Give it a rest, you crazy bastard! There's no one around. You shouted your lungs out last night.'

Then you break it off again. But she keeps coming back and you keep sending her away. You keep going out and meeting other women, harder women, less compassionate women. You go with them. You go home, impressed with their independence, impressed with the way they respond when you say you don't do relationships. 'Either do I,' they claim, and you think they might be okay to hang out with for a while, see what happens. Maybe it could turn into something. Maybe it could be something worthwhile. Maybe going out with someone who understands the need for space and a feeling of independence despite a partnership is just what you need. But in the morning after you take them home, after you drop them off, they look at you and in their eyes is that same hope, that same need, that same expression of a spider that, once the crap and the preliminaries of love are all done and dusted, installed as foundations for what is ultimately a ruse for breeding, will envelop you, feast on you, suck your blood, eat your life away and turn you into a puppetised shell of a man.

Stop it.

So stop it right there and then, before they end up crying, before they resemble that heartbreakingly sad face of your sister that one day of your life when you hit her, that train wreck memory when you wanted to say sorry but couldn't because you were a little boy, stubborn, unwise, proud, completely unaware that the next day she would be dead, completely unaware you would never get that chance to make her smile again, and you don't *ever* want to be reminded of *that* dark dark dungeon for as long as you live.

'Fuck them off!'

But still *she* is coming back. Still *she* will not let go. Now she's using legal means to hold onto *you*. Now she's claiming what is hers, your house, your family heirloom, your last effect from the previous dynasty of a family that's all done and dusted except you. Now *she* is ensuring her infiltration into this catalogue will be complete, and if you do not allow her in your world, to merge as if it is her rightful destiny, then she will take half your life, your soul, your infrastructure and eat it up like the female spider eating the male, and don't fight it because if you make her cry she will remind you of your past. And watch out for your DNA, watch out for your sperm. If she gets the chance she will take that too and implant it and then you *will* be tied to her forever and ever and ever and ever and ever and ever and ever and ever and EVER AND EVER AND EVER AND EVER AND EVER!

And you will *pay*. She will make you fucking *pay*.

'You happy now, you fuck? You happy you made me go nuts? Hey? You fuck. You fucking fuck. You fucking fuck, fuck, fuck.'

Biddie smiles. Biddie laughs. Biddie's enjoying the outburst he wanted, the reaction he always seeks for his entertainment, his escapism from the world he occupies and the boredom he suffers.

Lord, I hate my friends. Lord, I hate my life. And Lord, the bastard is right. I do hate myself.

'What did she tell you?' I ask, quietly, the echoes of my shouts still pinging about the shed, or my skull, or both.

Biddie's head wobbles. His mouth opens and it's wet, red, and gleeful.

'What's the difference?'

'Fuuuuucccccck yooooouuuuuu.'

I'm gonna break. I'm gonna shit myself. I'm gonna lose control and flip into madness. It's there. It's hovering. It's green and gooey. It's spread like a spider's web covered with scribblings and sketches and it's moving toward my eyes, my ears, my nose, my mouth, my face my face my face my face. I'm breaking. I'm over. I'm done. I'm thirsty.

'Hey guys,' says Rupert's urgent, whispering voice from a corner of the room.

'Fuck off,' I scream.

'Hey, shush. I'm just outside, okay?'

Startled, Biddie and I look in the direction of Rupert's voice. His shadow covers the light beaming through rust holes and we hear shoes crunching upon dry grass.

'What the hell are you doing here?' I say.

'Or more to the point, can you get us out of here?'

'Or more to the point, are those other guys around?'

We both look expectantly in Rupert's direction, glad we might get out of this alive, but even happier there's somebody here to finally break us apart.

'Nah, I don't think so. We've been looking around the place for a couple of hours, trying to find you. The Stanleys are in the next paddock, checking out a windmill. I was gonna go with them. Never thought they'd put anyone in here. How small is this *shed*?'

'Fucking tell me about it,' says Biddie.

'What are the Stanleys doing here?' The fear in my voice is palpable.

'Well, what happened, right, is after those bastards drove off with you and Biddie, I followed in Biddie's car, from a distance, right? Oh, and sorry Biddie, I crashed your car again. You don't have a passenger door anymore.'

'Rupert?' asks Biddie.

'Yeah?'

'Stop talking and get us out of here, okay?'

'Yeah, of course. So I followed them out here right, drove for like an hour or something, way out north, near, like, Dublin or something, and then they turned off into this farm, right? And so I didn't follow, 'cause I thought they would notice me, so I just kept going, and then I turned around and went back to the Stanleys. Fuck man, it took so fucking long. And then —

'Rupert, for fuck's sake,' Biddie says. 'Shut the fuck up and get us out of —

'Hey, you shut up, man. I didn't drive out here *twice* just to hear you talk to me like —

'Rupert, we're tied up and it stinks like Peter's shit.'

'I didn't shit myself. It's just vomit.'

'Just stop jabbering and open the fucking door.'

Rupert goes silent.

'Oh great. Good one, Biddie.'

He ignores me, but takes the venom from his voice. 'Rupert?'

There's no answer, and no footsteps in the grass.

'Rupert?'

There's still no answer.

'Great, fucking great,' I say. 'It was his fucking moment, man. He just saved us and you had to cut him down.'

Biddie ignores me but his jawbone flinches beneath his black sunglasses.

'Fuck, you're a self-righteous son-of-a-bitch,' I say.

Behind his sunglasses I imagine the stare of red, hateful eyes boring into my own.

'When we get out of here —

'Well you know the guy's sensitive. Why the hell do you have to —

'I'm not a baby, you know.'

It's Rupert's voice again and it's small and sad.

'Rupert, man,' I say. 'Don't worry about Biddie. It's just that we've been here for —

'And I'm not that fucking sensitive.'

'I know you're not, man. Biddie's just on edge, you see. He can't handle —

'And for your fucking information, right now I'm videoing you guys in that room, through this hole.'

He pauses for effect. Neither Biddie or I say anything.

'That's right. 'Cause what you guys don't know is this: this shit is *big*. That Jesus dude is all over the internet and I don't know what's going on but he ain't nothing special at all. Me and Pete worked *that* out, *Biddie*.'

'Rupert, you nutty fuck,' Biddie erupts. 'Why the fuck are you filming *us*?'

'Evidence, man.'

And at that moment, despite my vomit-filled mouth, despite the menacing end to a charade of a friendship with Biddie, despite the fact the last thing I drank was 10 beers and half a bottle of Scotch and my shrivelled face feels like a dog's arse, I could have kissed Rupert. I could have launched my body through the wall to hug his wiry, ratty frame. Because he *knows*. He knows this *matters*. He knows this kind of shit is wrong and we, the poor fucking buggers who landed in the middle of it, are the ones who have to do something about it.

'That's it, Rupert,' I say. 'Keep filming, man. You're a fucking legend, man. You're a fucking hero, and when you're done, we're gonna take our story to the media, man. We're gonna take it to them — and not the cops, man, don't worry about the cops, no fucking cops — and we're gonna expose this shit, man. We've got all that video from the scrub, right? We've got all that fucking around, and now we've got all this too. We're gonna fuck it up, man. You and me, we're gonna fuck it all up.'

Rupert doesn't respond.

'Great, you two do that,' says Biddie. 'But in the meantime, Rupert, please, pretty please, get me the fuck out of here!'

'Don't listen to him, Rupert. Don't listen to him. There's nothing wrong with you, man. You ain't nutty like Biddie says —

'Pah,' Biddie says.

'Just keep on filming, man. Just keep on getting that evidence. Film my arms, man. Film my legs. Get that sock on the ground. See that? It was forced into my mouth. I was gagged, man. I was gagged. Rupert? Rupert?'

The shadow at the hole has gone.

'Rupert?'

There's no footsteps, no shadow, no creak of a rusted tin door opening.

'Rupert!'

There's nothing at all, just the same silence we've been hating all night.

We sit quietly for a moment, straining to hear Rupert, but he's gone.

'Great. Fucking great,' I say. 'Well done, arsehole. You've killed us.'

'He'll be back,' Biddie says.

'You've fucking gone and killed us.'

'He'll be back!'

There's heavy steps in the grass outside. They circle our shed.

'Rupert?' I ask timidly.

Footsteps gather at the door behind me, followed by screeching metal and the brightness of white-hot sunlight streaming inside to curl my eyelids.

'Where's your friend?' says an unfamiliar voice.

'What?' I say, swinging my head around to a shadow at my shoulder. Swimming cornea dust hides his features.

'The little scrawny one, the one with the video camera.'

'What?' I ask again.

'Don't mess with us, mate. We don't have time and we won't mess about. Where is he?'

My adjusting eyes finally make out our visitors. The bulk and black outfits of the ex-FBI guys are unmistakable. There are three of them. One of them, the tallest, has a long nose and face, pointed ears, crew-cut hair and plain grey eyes that examine my face.

'What the hell's going on?' I say. 'Why the hell have you locked us away in here —

'Rupert's run off into the next paddock,' Biddie says.

'Shut up, man,' I hiss, looking at him in horror.

What's the difference? What's the difference? What's the difference?

'Is that so?' says the grinding voice of the tall guy.

'Don't listen to that snake,' I say.

'Bentley?' he says, turning to look at one of his cronies standing at the door. 'Go and look in the next paddock.'

The hulk of Bentley disappears from the door and more light pushes inside.

'Now then, what are we gonna do with you two?' the tall guy says.

'Hey, man,' Biddie says. 'None of this matters to me. I couldn't care less about what you guys are doing. This bastard stole my car. He's the one involved. He came to *me*.'

'Is that so?'

There are distant shouts outside.

'Lucas? Take a look outside and see what's going on.'

'He's right, you know,' I say to the tall guy as the second guy leaves. 'This piece of pissant shit in front of me doesn't give a shit about anything.'

'Yep, listen to that wanker,' Biddie's says. 'He's right.'

'Yep, I'm right. He's just an actor like your little Jesus fella. In fact, why don't you recruit him for your little show? Surely you can't use Jesus anymore, not after I busted up his face.'

'That was you, was it?'

'You're fucking right it was.'

'You know what?' the tall guy says, stepping between us as the shouting outside gets louder. 'You've caused a lot of trouble.'

'Good —

A teeth-busting hammer slams into my jaw. Lights explode in my face. I taste blood and brace for another hit, until one of his goons steps back inside the shed.

'Hey, Tyson. You'd better get out here.'

'What is it?'

'Just get out here. Now!'

The cries are close, getting closer, and familiar. There's no mistaking that howling dog.

'Shit,' Tyson spits as he ducks outside.

Rupert gets louder. I can hear the vibrato with every thump of his feet. He sounds like an excited kid playing cowboys and Indians.

'Who the hell are those guys?' we hear Lucas ask.

'Just get that camera,' says Tyson.

'Where the hell is Bentley?'

Moments later there are crashes outside, thuds, grunts, scuffling and swearing. A body slams against the left wall of the shed. The tin caves in a little. A fist connects with somebody's skin and bone. There's flapping in the dirt, trampling in dry grass, fingers grappling over the shoulders of hulking meat, clawing for leverage, panting, wheezing, bodies crumpling. There's a sickening *crack* and a body falls to the earth. It's followed by a distressed whinny that's silenced with a thud.

Biddie and I look at each other. We hear somebody run away.

'Get him,' Rupert shouts. 'Get that bastard. Don't let him get away.'

Relief washes over me.

'Rupert,' I yell.

A vibrating shadow enters the open light and Rupert stands between us, panting, spitting, gnashing his teeth. His eyes are wide, his hair sweaty, his clothes covered in brown grass and dried up paint. He looks at us and a smile, a beautiful child's smile, shines upon us both, banishing the dust and whatever's left of the gloom into the past. He holds Biddie's video camera up for us both to see.

'And I got the whole thing on camera.'

'Rupert, man,' I say. 'Untie us.'

'Sure thing, buddies.'

And he goes straight for Biddie, crouching behind his chair where the bastard's wrists are bound.

'What's going on out there?' I ask. 'How many of them are out there?'

'Only two, man,' Rupert says, wrestling with the rope. 'But that was enough. It always is.'

'Only two guys? There were three, man. There were three of them.'

'Only two Stanleys. How the hell do you untie this shit?'

'Use your fingernails,' Biddie says.

Rupert gives up on his fingers and takes to Biddie's bindings with his mouth. From my angle it looks a little dirty.

'Bet you'd like him to be doing that in front of ya, hey Biddie?'

'Fuck off.'

'That's it!' Rupert stops and stands up. 'I'm sick of you guys.'

He exits the shed but returns immediately with one of the Stanleys. He's even bigger than the ex-FBI guys. I hope it's not the one I offended yesterday.

'Now,' Rupert begins, scolding us like a fed-up child might scold his fighting parents. 'If either of you says anything even slightly negative, or even slightly fucked up, or even slightly agro to each other, Harold's gonna punch you. Right, Harold?'

Harold the Stanley nods his head before swinging it around — the neck of a dipping Diplodocus — into my face.

'Right,' he says.

Shit. It *is* the one I pissed off earlier. Just my fucking luck.

'Good job out there, Harold,' I say in a flattering voice. 'Bet those guys were a piece of piss for you, hey?'

'I just smash them all up,' he shrugs before nodding towards my nemesis.

'Biddie.'

'Harold.'

No question who's gonna get favoured here. Fucking Biddie and his cool guy attitude, why the hell does everyone like him? Why doesn't anybody see through his shit?

Harold the Stanley produces a hunting knife from his camouflaged cargo pants and steps behind a smug-looking Biddie to cut his bindings. Rupert steps towards the door.

'Ah, Rupert?' I say, my voice wavering as I imagine being left behind with a knife-wielding monster and a former friend who hates me.

'What?' He pauses at the entrance.

'How did you find us?'

With returning vigour he explains how he went back to the Stanleys from here and watched news footage of the guy I kidnapped addressing the TV — 'it must have been pre-recorded, man. There's no way' — while drinking the Stanleys' whiskey from plastic cups. He filled the Stanleys in on all that had happened in the day, or what he could remember of it — 'where did we get all those paint marks from, man?' — and they drove out here again, taking a stupidly long time for Rupert to find the turnoff, parking off the main road behind some bushes to start creeping about the farm. But it was dark. They didn't have any torches and the Stanleys didn't think it was a good idea to shout out for us, so they gave up, drove back home and went to sleep.

I wonder if Rupert powdered the Stanleys' feet first.

In the morning they came back and started looking once more, taking all morning to end up in our paddock. They never saw any of the vans or any of the ex-FBI thugs until now. They never saw anyone else on the farm at all. They weren't even going to check this shed until they heard me shouting.

And now Biddie and I are free, stretching our limbs outside the shed, rubbing our wrists, looking for water, stepping over and around two black and bloodied unconscious brutes with purple bruises on every visible section of their skin. Their empty black van sits silently with its doors ajar under a scraggly mallee tree to our left.

Two hundred metres away, where this paddock meets the next, the distant figure of the second Stanley makes his way towards us. He walks backwards, slowly dragging something heavy in the dirt. A wake of dust rises behind him, simmering in air that must be pushing to 30 degrees already. It causes the dust to pulsate haphazardly in a mirage that envelops the Stanley and his progress.

'I guess that's Bentley,' I say.

Harold the Stanley turns around to regard me. Even in the hot, bright sunlight, his eyes are black; the cavern inside his lips is black; the saliva wetting his teeth looks black.

'That's my brother.'

'No, I mean … the guy he's dragging, his name is Bentley.'

It computes inside Harold the Stanley's forehead. He returns to watching his brother whose name I still don't know.

'Pete,' Rupert says.

'Yeah?'

'Come with me.'

Rupert steps back into the shed and I follow him. Once inside he holds out a smartphone and taps his fingers on a greasy screen.

'You've gotta see this.'

We huddle over the phone waiting for a Channel 3 news page to load, but then an advert pops up to display various people jumping about to a jingle.

'Shoes, sneakers, heels and boots, Shiny Shoes has thongs to boot. Come inside, take your pick. Dance outside, embrace the heat.'

Rupert touches the screen again but it triggers a different advert, this time a tourism advert for the Adelaide Hills. We watch impatiently as two laughing couples with perfect hair, shiny teeth and designer sunglasses, buzz through European tree-filled valleys in a shiny SUV.

'Maybe hit that skip button,' I say, leaning forward to tap the screen. Rupert protectively moves the phone out the way so I hit the thumbnail of a waiting news report instead.

'Bloody hell, Rupert.'

'It's *Harold's* phone.'

'Channel 3 director Max Reaper has defended his network from fresh accusations of bias,' says a male newsreader, 'after photographs emerged on social media of him dining with Family Power candidate Tim Carling.'

'Is this what I'm meant to be watching?'

'Nah, I'm trying to show you that Jesus fella.' Rupert fiddles with the phone.

'The fact of the matter is,' says a white-haired man wearing a blue suit with sharp confidence, 'I'm friends with politicians from all walks of life, be they Tim Carling, Liberal members, Labor members, and even a few Greens, when they can pull themselves away from their soy lattes.' A pack of reporters holding microphones snigger. 'But my personal relationships do not alter Channel 3's commitment to factual, thorough, and unbiased news from all sides of politics. To suggest otherwise is, frankly, insulting.'

'This is the one.' Rupert holds the phone up. A different news report begins, this time narrated by a female newsreader as we watch phone footage of the fake Jesus at the beach.

'The Adelaide Archbishop has remained silent on a strange occurrence at Grange Beach this morning,' she says. 'In a scene reminiscent of bible stories, and captured with astonishing amateur footage, a man appeared on Grange Jetty moments after thousands of fish swarmed to the surface.'

The screen switches to different footage — steady and in high resolution — taken from what appears to have been a boat on the water. It shows the fake Jesus speaking briefly with a loud voice before disappearing into the sand dunes.

'That's pretty high quality for amateur footage,' I say.

'Isn't it?' Rupert says.

'One hour later,' the report continues, 'the man professing to be Jesus Christ reappeared at a football game in Adelaide's Parklands where he spoke with —

'Hang on. That's impossible! I had that bastard knocked out in the boot all *day*, man. And then we had him tied up in the hills 'til night time. There's no way that happened. No way.'

'No way,' Rupert agrees, nodding his head and eyeballing me.

'News of the event has spread quickly throughout Adelaide with church goers and non-church goers alike converging for spontaneous celebrations across the city.'

'Fucking turn it off, man. This is bullshit. It's fucking bullshit.'

Rupert taps the phone and puts it in his pocket.

'Those guys on that boat were there as back-up, man,' I say, following him outside, 'in case there wasn't enough phone footage from people on the beach, or it didn't look authentic enough. And there's no way everyone's bought it. They're using actors, man. They're all actors. Even those people at the beach —

I stop short. The Stanleys have arranged the three unconscious ex-FBI thugs to sit in a line against the side of the shed. Harold the Stanley stands next to his brother who holds a khaki bag in one hand — its weight made obvious by the bulging tendons in his forearm. They stare down at the three thugs in a strange, calculating fashion.

'What's going on?' I say.

Harold reaches into the khaki bag and pulls out a handgun. He aims it at the face of the tallest ex-FBI guy.

'No!' I scream, as flashes of trials, judges, gaol and rape hammer through my mind.

Pfft, pfft, pfft.

Three splodges of yellow paint explode and splatter across the faces and foreheads of Tyson, Bentley and Lucas.

'What the fuck is wrong with you people?' I scream, my heart beating a million kilometres an hour.

'Can I have a shot?' Rupert asks.

The Stanleys ignore him and tilt their heads in identical fashion as they assess Harold's accuracy. Tyson groans but doesn't wake up, his tongue licking at the paint on his face.

'You have got to be out of your fucking minds,' I shout. 'Do you even know what's going on around here? What the hell are you doing with paintball guns?'

The Stanleys turn their heads towards me with the same calculating expression of a moment ago. Harold raises the handgun and his twin brother reaches into the khaki bag. Rupert laughs nervously and steps between us, but then Biddie suddenly pulls up from the other side of the shed in his battered car.

'Can we get out of here now, please?' he says, looking at all of us and the ex-FBI thugs with disdain.

Harold lowers his paintball gun and crouches down to retrieve a set of keys from the side pocket of Tyson's black cargo pants, unhooking a carabineer that secures them to his belt. He walks away towards the black van. His twin brother steps towards Biddie's car, which, just as Rupert warned, is missing its front passenger door.

'Hang on,' Rupert says, hopping after the second Stanley. He reaches into the brute's khaki bag and pulls out a paintball rifle loaded with a canister of yellow paintballs. 'Okay, Pete. Let's go.' He runs towards Harold and the black van.

'Wait,' I shout. 'What about these guys?'

The thugs, slumped in the sun, seem to be melting, beads of sweat, blood and yellow paint sliding down their faces.

'Hey,' grunts the second Stanley, whose name I still don't know. He stands poised with one leg in Biddie's smashed up V6.

'Yeah?'

'Get the fuck out of here, you sad sack of shit.'

'Right.'

I follow Rupert towards Harold, who has already jumped into the driver's seat of the black van.

Phwok!

Yellow paint spreads in a disgorged star pattern across Labor candidate Justin Tomely's two dimensional face. It's the first election poster Rupert's actually hit.

'Whoo hoo!' he shouts triumphantly. 'Did you see that? I got him right between the eyes!'

The van hits a pothole and Rupert, half his body hanging outside its open sliding door, nearly slips to the road. He climbs back into the cabin, clutching the paintball assault rifle to his chest.

The back of Harold the Stanley's shiny bald head stares at us from the driver's seat up front as we fly along Port Wakefield Road, dissecting the dried paddocks and mallee trees on our way back to the city.

'Want a shot?' Rupert says, offering me the gun.

'For fuck's sake,' I shout, leaning forward so he can hear me over the wind created by the open door. 'Stop attracting attention.'

Harold leans out his own window and, with one hand on the steering wheel, fires off two rounds from his handgun at a blue Family Power poster as we approach it, one in the politician's forehead, the other in his throat.

Phwok phwok!

The candidate, Tim Carling, smiles like a car salesman through yellow paint as we pass.

'This is insane,' I shout. 'I've just been kidnapped and you idiots are shooting election posters?'

Rupert stands up and leans outside the door again, raising his rifle unsteadily to face more oncoming election posters mounted on stobie poles and farm fences alongside the highway.

'Hold my belt,' he shouts, the wind whipping his hair into a frenzy.

Pfft, pfft, pfft.

'Conserve your ammo,' Harold the Stanley barks. 'Aim before you shoot.'

Pfft … phwok!

Rupert loses his balance again and I lurch forward to grab his belt, pulling him back and pushing him to the floor of the van.

'You crazy bastard. You're leaving a trail of paintballs all the way back to the shed.'

I point to the road behind us where Biddie and the other Stanley are following in his beaten up V6.

'You're right.' Rupert puts the gun down. 'It's just a bit of fun anyway. Here.' He retrieves the video camera from the seat and holds it out to me. 'Take this.'

'Why? It's your movie.'

'Nah, I mean, take it. And don't let Biddie see.'

'Okay,' I say warily. 'But you're the one who's been doing all the filming. Why stop now?'

Rupert giggles briefly before putting a hand quickly over his mouth to suppress it. He regards me with wide eyes over the top of his hand. They might be excited but they're also exhausted and show the wrinkles of crows' feet.

'I'm not going on with this.'

'What'd you mean you're not going on with this? You rescued us. You came and brought the cavalry, man. You're the hero.'

'That's not … ' Rupert drops his hand from his mouth. 'Alright, yeah, that was pretty cool, wasn't it? And we KO'ed those dudes, man. We fucked 'em right up. You should'a seen it. It's all on the camera anyway.'

'That's it, man, as well as all the other stuff. We've gotta expose this shit. We've gotta take it all to the media.'

'Yeah, the media has to get it,' he says unconvincingly.

'Hey. Don't back out on me now, man. It's gotta be done.'

'Yeah, it's gotta be done.' But his assertion is barely a murmur.

'C'mon, man. Everyone's so full of shit these days. Everyone's taking everybody for a ride. Everyone's swallowing down this … this … fucking consumer age, buy everything, do your fucking hair, wax your legs before you're even fucking twelve, and pompous on everyone in your fucking piggy fucking way and —

'Pete, man —

'You know what I'm saying, man. This whole fucking city is screwed, man. It's fucking rooted and no one does anything about it but then they go and pull this shit. They go and fake the Second Coming of a guy who, you said so yourself, was a great man, a bloke who'd hate all of this shit and would probably flush it away like the pig shit it is. They go and get some fucking actor from some fucking —

'Pete, shut the fuck —

' — actor school in Sydney, who doesn't have the first clue what —

'Man, you *do* sound like me. Just like Biddie said.'

'What?' The accusation stuns me for a moment. 'Fuck what Biddie says. It doesn't matter. This is real, man, and I don't care who I sound like. This ain't no fucking conspiracy. You know it. This is the real fucking deal and you and I have to do something about it. You and me.'

Rupert slowly nods his head.

'I'm not going with you, man,' he says, still nodding.

'Why?'

'It's too heavy.'

'That's right, it *is* heavy. That's why we've gotta do it together. That's why —

'Biddie's right. I'm only going to screw it up for ya.'

'What? No, listen. About Biddie, he sold you out to save his own skin. He's a fucking snake.'

'I don't care.'

'He told those guys where you were, and he sold me out. He sold us both out.'

'It doesn't matter.'

'Yeah, it does. Listen, man. The guy's a —'

'I know, alright? I fucking know.'

Phwok Phwok!

Harold executes another 2D politician with assassin-like precision, this time a Liberal candidate called Candice Charleston with blonde curls. I cringe, imagining cops pulling us over any minute, throwing firearms laws at us, the stolen van, my assault, the kidnapping of the fake Jesus.

'Just take it,' Rupert says, holding out the camera. 'This is *your* thing.'

'No —'

'C'mon, let's face the truth here. You're better than me —'

'Don't listen to —'

'Shut up!'

I hold my tongue.

'The thing is … you disappoint me too.'

'Wha —'

'You're wasting your brain, man. You drink too much. You should be doing something else.'

My teeth clench. I can feel my face going red, my anger stretching bitter wings.

'Just take the camera, Pete, and go see it to the end.' Rupert throws the camera onto the seat next to me and picks up his paintball gun.

'You son of a —'

'None of us are gonna help ya. The Stanleys won't. They don't like you.' He leans out the door and shoots at an election poster for The Greens, a hipster with a cropped beard, but misses entirely. 'Biddie won't 'cause he doesn't care.'

'Biddie's a selfish old fuck.'

'And I won't 'cause I'm only gonna fuck it up for ya, and this is far too serious.'

Pfft, pfft, Phwok. Candice Charleston gets one in the neck.

'Fuck that, man. You're not leaving me alone with this. Now shut up and let's get this camera to the media, you and me.'

Phlap phlap!

Rupert abruptly lurches backwards and bangs his head on the doorframe. His gun clatters to the floor as he clutches his face. Yellow paint drips from his black hair and over his cheeks.

I turn about to see the second Stanley hanging outside the window of Biddie's car behind us, laughing, a paintball assault rifle in his own hand, Biddie sneering alongside him in the driver's seat.

Rupert retreats onto his seat with a hurt expression on his face. I watch him for a moment, both our bodies swaying with the momentum of the van as we hurtle towards the city. We pass a dried salt lake shimmering in the sun. It looks like it hasn't had water in years, the surface of albino Mars. It gives way to rows of glasshouses, some new, some old, some with accompanying houses sitting quietly among mallee trees and wrecked cars. A series of shiny billboards interrupt the scene with adverts for a new housing estate surrounded by green paddocks and manmade lakes.

'Sustainable living. Green lifestyle. Lake View Estate — coming soon.'

A crosswind gust blows topsoil through our open sliding door.

'You know what?' I say, leaning forward and talking into Rupert's ear. '*You* don't need *those* guys. You're better than that, man. You're better than all of them.'

'You don't know anything about that, Pete,' he murmurs, wiping yellow paint from his eyes. 'The Stanleys are okay. They just … they're a bit like you.' He coughs. 'No dad.'

It stings worse than his accusations of useless alcoholism only moments ago. I look at Harold. He remains impassive and huge at the front of the van.

'They're nothing like me,' I say, shaking my head. 'They've got a mum.'

'That's where we're going now. I've never met her before, but … ' Rupert leans forwards and whispers, his tired green eyes accentuated by the yellow paint over his face. 'I don't think she did much for them.'

'What?' I say a little too loudly. 'What the hell are we going to their mum's for? We've gotta get to Channel 3 or something, man. We've gotta take this shit straight to the media.'

'Biddie can't drive his car into town like that. We've gotta get rid of all that paint and fix his door.'

'Fuck Biddie. And fuck their mum. This is bigger than both of them. It's bigger than all of —

Phwok!

'Ow!' I shout, clutching my knee where an explosion of paint stings. I look up in time to see Harold the Stanley — twisted around in his seat — change his aim to my other knee.

Phwok!

'Ow! Shit. Watch the road, for fuck's sake!'

But the van is no longer moving. We've pulled over onto the side of the road. And the Stanley is looking at me from the front with a horrible look in his black eyes. They don't even shift as a road train roars past us, disrupting air so it slams into our van and makes it wobble. Rupert picks up his paintball gun and jumps out the van through the sliding door.

'Rupert,' I shout, but he disappears. The Stanley's figure seems to swell and fill the entire front section of the van, his eyes two black pits of terrible nothing.

'S … sorry,' I stammer. 'I didn't mean to say anything about your mum. I just … I just think this is too important to be fucking around, I mean, messing around, with.'

His fist creaks like hardened leather around the hilt of his gun. My fingers crawl across my seat and find the video camera.

'You know what?' I croak. 'I think I'll just do this thing on my own after all. I'll just get a cab from here.'

'No,' Harold says with his strangely distorted voice that seems to come from another world. 'This is the end of the line for you.'

My insides suck inwards. He raises an arm, but rather than reach out to crush my skull, the Stanley points past me and out the door. I turn warily and see a line of tall gum trees lining what must be a creek heading away from the highway. An unsealed access road follows alongside it. It leads to a dirty clump of glasshouses and an old farmhouse.

'That's my mum's place. And if you don't wanna go over and explain how you'd like to "fuck her", then you'd better shut the fuck up, and get out of here, you sad sack of shit.'

My mouth opens to retort but then it clicks. The Stanleys have been dealing dope ever since they came to Blackwood and here, on the Northern Plains, the plastic glasshouses are renowned for growing weed. Nobody talks about it though, because the Northern Plains are also where people disappear.

'Right,' I say. Harold turns and disembarks from the van. Rupert pops his head around the sliding door.

'All good?' he says cheerfully.

I want to put my fist through his stupid looking face.

'Where the fuck did you go?'

'We're going with Biddie,' he continues. 'You can take the van, and good luck, man. Do us proud.'

'Do us proud?' I spit. 'What is this fucking moment? The fucking "suddenly-you're-in-the-fucking-Olympics-motherfucker-so-do-us-all-proud" fucking moment?'

'Something like that. See ya, Pete.'

Rupert bounds away, leaving me alone inside the van with Biddie's camera.

'Fuck this,' I shout. 'I ain't gonna do a damn thing either. I'm just gonna go home and get drunk. Just like you. I'm gonna do nothing like you.'

I jump out of the van but it's too late. Rupert's already sitting in Biddie's car with the others. He waves from the back seat as they accelerate off the road shoulder, a wheel rubbing against a broken mudguard, various components of machinery scraping the bitumen beneath.

The beaten-up car turns off the highway to clatter up the access track and I suddenly feel hopelessly alone.

"The following rant was left for me by Peter Mackay on our dining room table approximately one week before separation." LT

Why not go back to Uni, you say. Why not finish your honours and go into academia? Aca-aca-demia. I have such POTENTIAL, you say. It's so disappointing to see me WASTE my LIFE. What's wrong, Leanne? A boyfriend working in a pizza shop isn't good enough? You're so damned fussy about what you eat.

But it isn't the pizza that makes you fat. It's your phone, your NETFLIX, your Instagram PICS and sarcastic GIFs, the Facebook arguments that captivate you like a car crash. News, opinion, fake lives and click BAIT, it fattens you up, marinates, cooks for consumption, anything that happens anywhere forced down your throat like ice-cream, the latest arsehole acting like a CUNT, the latest bitch acting like a PRICK, the latest BINGE series, the latest celebrity fuck-up, the economy GOD and INTEREST rates.

Rupert got rid of his phone, said it was information overload, said everyone's a drone plugged into a communal think tank. I reckon he's wrong. I reckon it gives us shit to think about, people to hate, MISOGYNISTS, graffiti artists, dole bludgers, fucking HOON DRIVERS. BURN them like diseased COWS.

Fuck them up with IRONIC memes, with non-contextual QUOTES, on our laptops, our phones, our anti-Christ Dick Tracy fucking smartwatches.

It's a City of Judgement, Leanne, and we must hate who it hates, love who it loves, be who it WANTS US TO BE. Because if you don't, if you won't suck on its digital cock, swallow or spit its algorithmic shit, then die, piss off, you're a trouble maker, a weirdo, a pretentious twat and you're definitely no fucking AUSSIE BATTLER.

Tell me what's going on, you say. What have I been thinking? I tried but it's like talking to a toothbrush. You act clean but you stink of plaque. I prefer your garden gnome. It's ceramic but not as rotten.

I'm heading out with Rupert. Call me if you want but I probably won't answer.

The highway growls beneath the black van's wheels. The dashboard is modern with green-lit consoles. Air-conditioning fans my face, cools my skin, sends a much-needed breeze over my skull.

Cars dawdle before me driving 10kph below the speed limit but I don't attack. I sit back and listen to Rupert in my head: 'You disappoint me too'.

I had career prospects. I got drunk and ruined them all. I had friends who became successful, got hooked up, forged a future, had babies. They stopped calling me years ago. I had a woman who loved me, who was beautiful, who was decent and kind and clever. I chopped her heart with a cleaver.

Abandoned paddocks fling past on either side of the van, brown and dead. On the side of the road little food houses, and fresh fruit outlets, appear and disappear. Service stations loom, pass, make space for other service stations that loom and pass, and all the time buildings and shops and houses become more frequent, more and more congested, as the city nears.

Leanne loved me. That's why she repulsed me, because how can you respect someone who loves what you hate?

Smiling politicians on blue election posters stare down at me from stobie poles. Blackboard stands sit on the road's shoulder: 'Bananas: $2.99 a kilo', 'Five mangos for $4', 'Justin Tomely for Wakefield', 'Vote Liberal', 'Jesus lives!'

Not here he doesn't, not in my body, not in my soul. A great man he may have been, but he sure as shit isn't here now.

'Biddie's right.'

Fuck off, Rupert. What the hell would Biddie know?

I remember the night Leanne and I visited him after Nan's funeral. I was the central act, sitting in front of two sober spectators, drinking like there was no tomorrow, sculling the beers and burping freely, aggressively, washing down the image of my last remaining relative, her made-up face a horizontal façade of still life reeking from her casket — perfumed, rosy — yet lifeless, abhorrent, finished.

We sat on Biddie's back porch while I drank and attempted conversation. Biddie answered politely but made no effort to draw things out. Leanne sat with a worried expression on her face — her green eyes warped by a constant frown that squeezed them down.

'Well, at least Nan's out of that damned nursing home,' I said to Biddie. 'They say it's God's waiting room, and fuck man, isn't that the truth.'

'Yeah, I've heard them say that,' Biddie said, looking away.

'But what else are you gonna do? Hey? You get old, it's where you've gotta go. What else can people do?'

'Pete,' Leanne started.

'And besides, that lot ought to think they're lucky. They made it old enough to go into a home. Not many ... Not many make it. Fuck, you know what I mean.'

I stared at Biddie.

You *know* what I mean.

I searched his face, looking for understanding, searching for solidarity, wanting empathy from a friend I'd known most of my life. I'd come for that purpose. Leanne was driving me nuts. Her fretful face, her worried eyes, her damned tears at the funeral — wet and warm, pattering on my shoulder as Nan's casket trundled off on a conveyor belt. They were for display. I could tell by the way she looked at me to make sure I noticed them as my lineage was sucked away. Leanne wanted me to notice her sadness, notice her devotion, remember that she was *there* the day my family finally evaporated.

I sought Biddie's support because I knew it wouldn't come with an agenda like it did with Leanne.

But he didn't respond. He just nodded and looked at Leanne.

'You're driving, right?'

'Yeah, she's fucking driving,' I blurted out, the sound of my voice seeming to hover in the air.

'Chill, man,' Biddie said, putting his hand on *Leanne's* shoulder to stop her coming to me. 'It's rough, okay? You're doing it rough.'

'Yeah, it's rough,' I repeated. 'It's fucking rough.'

I tipped a beer down my throat and burped.

'Leanne, maybe you need to take him home.'

'Hey, man,' I started. 'I came here to get away from her, you fuck.' No one spoke. 'Fuck it, I'm taking a piss.'

I stood up and knocked over my plastic chair, stumbling off the porch into the night air. I didn't know why I was so angry, why I felt so betrayed, but when a murmur of conversation resumed as I walked away, I called taxi and left.

'Why are you dwelling in such a shadowy cloud?' Leanne said a week later, stroking my bottom lip as she passed to the kitchen.

She refused to take my behaviour to heart. It was just grief, as far as she was concerned, and it didn't have to affect her rose-scented world. She maintained that attitude right until the end when I started walking out every night, when my brooding, acid-laden fog began stretching over her ideals with insidious wretchedness.

Dammit, Leanne. Couldn't you see what was happening?

The road throws onwards. The fields give way to factories, car yards with empty spaces and the occasional social services outlet. Ahead is an octagonal church with a steeple at its centre. On the footpath facing the road, young people hold a brightly painted banner and jump up and down to attract attention.

'JESUS HAS RETURNED!' the banner reads.

And the lies will continue. The deceit will remain. The pigs who surround me and who are better than me will follow in the footsteps of idiocy and swill the bullshit so fast they miss the taste.

I wind down my window and lean my head out.

'It's a fucking lie,' I shout.

The kids look at me startled. My eyes lock with those of a boy with black hair. He doesn't like what he sees.

'You fucking taste it too,' I spit at him as my van passes.

The city draws near. There are welcome signs on the road. There are more billboards. Home-grown beer, wine, shopping centres, sport, more shopping centres, more beer adverts — witty, cool, directed to everyone, our vices advertised as if they were harmless, as if they were natural, as if they would never ruin anyone.

'Support your patch. Drink local,' reads one sign above a picture of a tradie sitting at a bar by himself.

'The Barossa. Lose yourself,' reads another with a picture of a woman lying in the dirt wearing what looks like a nightie.

I pass new housing estates, property developments, latest amenity-filled trendy boxes with gutter-to-gutter roofing and tiny rubber-lawn backyards. They're a face covered with acute acne, a condition spreading over the city's outskirts.

I enter the realm of traffic lights, crossroads, industry and snail-pace driving. A huge piece of fabric with words painted upon it in bright pink flaps about on a car yard's road-facing fences.

'The drought has broken. Jesus is here!'

I want to drive the van like a torpedo straight into it. Instead I grit my teeth and pass this monument to all things stupid, to those who wait for simple solutions and somebody else to come and extract them from their mess. I turn my cheek from this sign that, even now, reaches into my soul, twists it into rage, makes me want to track down the bastards who caused this latest insult to rationality, the pricks who made a —

'He was a great man. He did great things,' says Rupert.

— mockery of whatever God may or may not be, the man who accepted hideous torture to become the greatest, most famous martyr of all time.

'The original revolutionary, man!'

Shut the fuck up, Rupert.

I pass this travesty, and as I do so, my teeth grinding, my newly growing shoots of understanding drying up and crumbling apart, I see faces in the cars travelling in the opposite direction. They smile triumphantly and point at the sign before beeping their horns in a show of support.

I stick my head out my window.

'Shut the fuck up, you stupid fucking gutless fucks.'

News spreads fast. The bastards behind this had it planned. The 'Coming' was only the opening act. This buzz was prepped and primed weeks ago. I assumed Rupert had been exaggerating, but not this time.

I look at Biddie's camera again, remembering the high quality footage from the beach, wondering suddenly if the media was in on it, remembering another one of Rupert's rants.

'The media's all controlled, man. It's all censored. It's all run by the *man*, man. You see nothing without his approval.'

A red light draws traffic to a stop. An oversized SUV pulls up in the lane next to me. A nice-looking lady in the passenger seat turns to look at me, smiles, and waves. I wave back, but I don't smile. I wind down my window. She does the same, smiling even more broadly.

'Hi,' she says. The driver — her husband, I suppose — turns to look at me with a smile that matches her own. They must have been together for some time. Their facial muscles have replicated.

'Do we know each other?' I say.

They both laugh.

'I don't think so,' she says.

'Then what are you smiling at?'

'Haven't you heard?' she laughs heartily, guiltlessly.

'We're all family now, my friend,' says her husband.

'What?'

The lights turn green, but we remain stationary. I wait for an irritated honk from behind us.

'Jesus has returned,' the woman continues with a gracious shake of her head. 'We're all saved.'

'But … ' I start. They wait for me to continue, smiling earnestly. Still nobody beeps. I look in the rear-view at the driver behind me. He should be gesticulating angrily, motioning for me to move on. Instead he catches my eye and merely raises an eyebrow in question.

'But you *believe* it?' I ask warily, returning my gaze to the couple.

'Son,' the man says. 'Turn on the news.'

'He's been performing *miracles*,' his wife says.

'Oh, for fuck's sake.'

The lady frowns. At that moment a shadow enters my peripheral vision.

'Do you think you folks could get moving?'

Startled, I look up at the face of a man who has come to stand next to my van. It's the driver of the car behind me.

'The light did go green some time ago.'

'Why didn't you just beep the horn?' I ask.

'Oh,' the man chuckles, looking at the couple in the car. 'I don't think that's necessary on such a wonderful day like today.'

The couple laugh with him and smile knowingly at each other.

'Has everyone in this place gone fucking mad?'

'But,' says the man on the road with a troubled look. 'Haven't you been watching the news?'

'No, I haven't been watching the fucking news. I've been tied up in a shed out in whoop-whoop by dudes in black who are running this whole fucking show and, even if I was at home, I smashed my TV last weekend.'

'What about …' says the women gingerly. 'What about your phone?'

'I smashed that too, but you lot had all better keep yours because by teatime tonight you're gonna have a lot of egg on your daft fucking faces.'

I extend my arm out the window, slap the driver's face, and put my foot down on the accelerator to zoom out of their world.

'Motherfucker,' I exclaim to the car. 'This is ridiculous.'

How can they just believe it? How can they not even question it?

I glance at the radio in the centre of the van's dashboard, half expecting it to smash me with a series of adverts about beach towels, reality TV and dancing shoes. It doesn't. I'm about to turn it on to seek news about the fake Jesus when I freeze at a new sight. A string of caravans and cars laden with camping equipment are lined up waiting to enter a large paddock on the other side of the highway. A makeshift sign has been erected; 'Camp Resurrection' it reads in fresh blue paint. I slow the van to a crawl. It looks like a carnival, day one of a camp-out music festival decorated with signs and banners that read 'Jesus Lives' or 'Christ has returned' and even 'The end is nigh'. Here and there I see an Australian flag standing erect and proud in the shimmering sun, a British flag or two, an Italian flag like the one in the shop window at work, but mostly blue flags proclaiming 'Power and Life' in a bold white font, dozens of them. I see a flatback truck with a five-piece band playing music to a small group of young adults and children who hop about excitedly near the entrance. I see car after car, caravan after caravan, lined up waiting to enter the village, people milling about and talking on the road, coffee vans, icecream vans, then I pass three giant motor homes in succession, each of them flying an oversized American flag from their bonnets.

'You've got to be kidding me,' I say, mesmerised, slowing down.

A group of people stand next to four cars parked ahead of me on my side of the road. As I draw near, a couple cross the road from the line of pilgrims and approach them. A man with scruffy hair and an ugly moustache holds his hand over his heart and smiles at them. A blonde woman wearing stonewashed jeans extends her arms as if she's going to embrace them.

I open the van's windows as I approach.

'But isn't it beautiful?' The man with the moustache is saying. 'Can't you just accept the miracle and enjoy the beauty of it —

'Are you people for real?' interjects a young woman from the group. 'You can't possibly believe this shit.'

'Why?' her friend says with his arms crossed. ''Cause you saw it on the internet?'

'My sentiments exactly,' I shout, swerving the car towards the two pilgrims, making them jump off the road as I burn away. Moments later I overtake a small busload of drunks on their way back from the Barossa hurling abuse at believers from its windows.

Fucking news, fucking information overload. But at least some of us are fighting. And if I'm gonna do anything about this travesty

I've involved myself in, then I need to know what's going on. I need to know what the pigs have been fed.

I push buttons on the radio's face to hear the news. Green lights come on and I brace myself for advertising.

Instead there is static. It coughs. There is more static, then there is a voice:

'Roger that.'

Roger what?

The static returns, followed by another cough.

'Alpha Three, please report. Has the video camera been acquired?"

With one hand on the wheel I lean down to look at the centre dashboard. Just above my left knee hangs a handheld mouthpiece, connected to a radio transmitter with coiled black wire. It wiggles slightly with the motion of the van.

'Alpha Three, if you're receiving please reply.'

I reach down to unclip the mouthpiece, planning to give the professional bastards something to receive, but cogs in my mind whirr into action.

'Evidence, man,' Rupert's voice reminds me.

Still driving with one hand, I reach over to the passenger seat, pick up Biddie's video camera, turn it on and record the radio face.

'Alpha Three. Please report. Have you acquired the video camera? … Shit.'

Static. There's a cough and then a new voice speaks.

'There will be shit if you don't get that camera.'

The static stretches on for a moment before the original voice speaks again.

'Tyson's crew went out to the farm for intel, sir.'

'Where are they?'

'Alpha Three still hasn't reported in, sir.'

'Yes, I know that. There's a man here before me who is none too pleased, Alpha Two.'

'Roger that, sir.'

'What are you going to do about it, Alpha Two?'

'Sir, my team will visit the farm if Alpha Three doesn't check in by 1300.'

'We don't have time for this.'

'Roger that.'

'Event Four is scheduled for 1800.'

'Roger that.'

'For fuck's sake, get your arse out to the farm now. Something's gone wrong.'

'Sir, Tyson's crew are A-one. They'll have it under control.'

'Is it under control now, Alpha Two?'

'Sir, that's hard to discern without contact from Alpha Three.'

'Was it under control last night, Alpha Two?'

'No, sir. That guy made a lot of noise. He placed the whole operation in jeopardy. If we had pursued, the subject could have been seen.'

'Is the operation in jeopardy now, Alpha Two?'

'Sir, if we give Alpha Three more time, I'm sure they'll have it under control.'

'Dimwit.'

Static.

'Roger that.'

'Alpha Two, Alpha Three is *not* in control. Get your arse out to the farm, find out what's happened, get the camera, and meet us here at 1430.'

'Roger that. Sir, what is your location?'

'Dimwit! The Outlet. Out.'

'Roger that. Out.'

Static.

'Alpha Three, this is Alpha Two. Do you copy? ... Shit.'

My brain rattles with questions. The Outlet, what's that? And what the hell is Event Four? The 'Coming' on the beach must have been Event One. Two and Three must have happened while we were imprisoned. Something big was about to happen.

'What's the difference?'

'Shut up, Biddie,' I say aloud. 'This is big. This is real. Those *believers* of the biggest lie this city ever committed, I've gotta help them. I've gotta show them they've been swindled and help get them back on track.'

Back on track to what?

Back on track to just beeping the fucking horn when someone's in your way.

I flatten the accelerator with my foot.

'I wish you would just tell me what's going on with you,' she said, her eyes wet.

'Do you ever *think*, Leanne? You know, like ever really *think*?'

A shiny modern car slows in front of me. I tailgate it for a moment, just to make sure the driver's aware of me, that I'm inconvenienced, and change into the overtaking lane.

'Of course I think, and lately …' She trailed off, deliberately, for effect, for drama. 'Lately, all I've been thinking of is you.'

Leanne looked me squarely in the eye at that point, wanting my sympathy, wanting me to think about her.

'That's not thinking. You're not thinking. You're acting. You're reacting. I'm trying to talk to you about *stuff* and all you're doing is thinking about us, and me, and you and I, and what it all means to you. That's not what I meant. I said, do you ever think, like really ever *think*?'

Her green eyes welled up, her lips trembled and I couldn't help but think of the feral rabbits we caught in a trap once when I was a kid on a scout camp. There were no adults about so my friends and I had to destroy them ourselves — only they wouldn't die. We tried to cut their throats. They squealed and wailed horribly, but the fur was thick and we couldn't penetrate the windpipe with our blunt pocket knives. We kicked them in the head, but they wouldn't go unconscious. We picked up one of the metal traps and smashed their skulls. Their eyes expanded and bulged out of their heads, hanging by tendons, but they wouldn't stop kicking their legs and the blood didn't flow. It just matted their fur from their mouths where we hit them, their noses where we stabbed them, their hopelessly slashed throats and busted ears, but still they wouldn't die. They just made a noise, a horribly discordant squealing, and their eyes, dangling from their sockets, looked at us in the torchlight, never turning away, in fear, in shock, in trembling, unadulterated horror, and Leanne's eyes looked the same. She wasn't listening to me. She only feared that I would leave her, that the future she'd imagined for herself would be cancelled. It made me feel that love is cheap, irrational, hormone driven, and we are nothing but bunny rabbits hoping for safety and a warm place where we don't have to think. We're not allowed to think. We don't want to think.

I pull up to within centimetres of a ute travelling a little under 80kph in the fast lane.

'Motherfucker.' I flash my headlights. 'Get the fuck out of the overtaking lane.'

'What's that supposed to mean, Peter? What do you want me to think about?'

She didn't understand. Her tears showed she'd never get it. It was only us in her mind, only our relationship and all the trappings of a partnership she saw falling apart.

'Ah, forget it,' I said.

'No,' Leanne said in her strong, stubbornly defiant way. 'I want to understand, Peter. Please, please tell me.'

The driver of the ute gets the message and speeds up. He overtakes the car in the left lane, puts on his indicators, and changes into the lane to let me by.

'Don't you think, this entire little world we live in down here, don't you think it's, it's … I don't know, kind of plastic? Don't you ever take a look at yourself and think, wow, I'm just another piece of plastic in LEGOLAND City doing all the same LEGOLAND things that all the other pieces are doing, and none of it's really good. Like, you know, nothing we do is *good*.'

Her eyes were so wide I could see her soul. But it wasn't analysing my words. It was analysing *me*.

I look at the driver ute as I pass.

He smiles and waves.

'Wake up,' I scream.

'What isn't good about us?' she asked.

'What isn't good?' I replied indignantly, as if she should know, as if it should be common knowledge and in her face at all times. 'Leanne, have you been paying attention? Our world is on the brink, and us, us, you and me, and everyone we know and everything we've done and everything we do, are the cause of it. We are the cause of it. Don't you ever wonder about that? I mean, what the hell are we, some kind of virus taking over the planet to suffocate it? Look at us. We've spread like a disease, whitey taking over blacky, whitey spreading over everything, whitey raping and pillaging and stealing and destroying and using and abusing and now it's all crashing. Now it's all falling apart, and you, and us, and everyone here, all we do is keep going the same way. We don't change anything, not for real. We talk and talk and talk, and people talk like they're doing something, but ultimately all we care about is us, and our home, and our fucking relationship and what fucking couch we should buy for the house my dead Nan gave to us.'

'Well, what should we do?' Leanne snapped. 'Pack up and head to … to Uganda or something to work in an orphanage? Or maybe we should go to Sweden and sit on the steps with Greta Thunberg? I'm not going anywhere. My family's here.'

'Fuck your family.'

And I didn't mean that, but out it came and it was done.

'Uh!' Leanne said with surprise, with indignation, with the first real hint of the anger I would see for the rest of days. 'How dare you.'

'Fuck everyone's families. We're all doing the same thing. We're all the same problem. It's just that everyone's programmed to think that theirs is so uniquely special, that their own family is so uniquely important, that supplying the cars, the clothes, the food, wine and recreation is so inherently our right, that we don't stop. No one ever stops. But don't you ever *think*, Leanne? Don't you ever think that your family is not so important, that your family is not worth the endless drain on everything, that we've all got to stop breeding new families and start worrying about the ones that are starving? At least until we finish it all off with World War Three or even Four over the last bits of oil, or the last drops of rain, or the last fillets of fish.'

'That's not going to happen.'

Bitch.

'And who are you to even talk about families?' she continued. 'You don't even have one.'

'Shut up.'

'And if they were still here today —

'Shut up.'

'If someone else as well as you survived that car crash —

'Don't say it.'

'Then they would be disgusted with you. They would be ashamed. How dare you? Who the hell do you think you are?'

I wanted to slap her but I didn't. I've never hit a girl in my life, except my sister that one time, but that was when we were both little enough to fight over a stupid lollypop. She died the next day so it doesn't count.

But it does. It always does. Scarlet upon white, it never stops.

I'm near the city centre. The traffic has stopped at another red light.

'Leanne?' I say to the air between me and the windshield. 'I'll tell you one thing. I bet *they* knew what it was like to think, right at the moment that stupid maniac cut us off and smashed us to bits. I bet my mum and dad thought more at that moment as death cut open their eyes with broken glass than you will ever think in your stupid, happy, bunny rabbit life.'

She sobbed. She sniffed. She looked at me with juicy, salt-water covered eyeballs.

'Bunny rabbit what?'

A large LED sign flashes from the side of the road. 'Get your online Channel 3 subscription now and save,' it reads, before blinking and showing the time and temperature: '12:58pm. 35°C'. And it's meant to be the middle of winter.

She realised we were over.

I realise I'm in the wrong lane. The flashing LED sign is now pointing towards a brand new Channel 3 TV station on the left.

I put on my indicator and prepare to muscle into the exit lane, but the driver of a car slows to allow me in.

'Fuck you,' I shout as I pass, extending my middle finger before turning onto Channel 3's street and stopping. In my rear-view the driver of the car I just insulted, an obese lady in her forties, smiles and pulls up behind me. The other lane is free, but she won't pull out and go around me. She waits.

'C'mon, fucking do something,' I say to her face in the mirror, before turning my attention to the Channel 3 building. It's shiny, eight stories high, and covered in branding.

I feel Rupert prod me in the ribs.

'This is *your* thing,' he says.

In my rear-mirror there's a tiny frown on the lady's face. Finally, she tries to pull around me into the next lane, but I accelerate immediately and stop in front of her. Wheels squeal as she brakes. She raises her hands and glares at my face's reflection with agitation.

I get out the van and walk towards her car. She frantically locks her doors. I reach her door and gently tap on the pane.

'Hello,' I say. 'What are you scared of? Don't you know that Jesus has returned?'

She looks at me hopefully for a moment, before noticing my mouth, my clenched teeth, and slams her car into reverse.

'If you truly believe Jesus is here, then what the hell are you scared of?' I shout after her. 'Where's your faith? Hey? Where's your fucking faith?'

Another car coming down the road swerves to avoid her.

'Why are you so hateful?' said Leanne another day.

'Get the fuck out of my life,' I said on another.

Out the front of the TV station, two men and a woman stand watching me, all wearing suits. Above them a bright red plastic '3' shines from the wall.

'Hi,' I shout, waving at them. 'I've got something for you. Wait there.'

I run back to the van and open the passenger door.

The girl whoops in fright. A man shouts, 'No', and all three run back inside.

'No, no, no,' I shout at the closing glass doors. 'It's just a video camera.'

I pluck it from the idling van and hold it high in the air. 'See? Just a video camera.'

I cross the road and walk through a stylised, minimalist street garden, holding the video camera above my head like a hunter returned with his kill.

'It's nothing to be scared of, and I've got something for you. Man, have I *got* something for you. It's the story of the year, the story of the decade.'

Reaching the automatic doors, I wait for them to open but they don't. I can see the three suits standing in the foyer, watching me.

'Hey, check this out. I've got some crazy footage for you. It's about this Jesus stuff. C'mon, open the door.'

A security guard appears from a shadow and walks towards the door. One hand rests upon the gun at his belt.

'Oh, c'mon, man. There's no need for that. Look in my hand here, look. It's a video camera. It's important. That Jesus is fake. I've got proof. It's right here. Look.'

The security guard shakes his head, but one of the suits, the youngest of the men, approaches the guard and they talk. They both look at me for a moment, until the young guy walks to the door, reaches up, and pushes a button hidden from view. The glass doors slide open and cool air escapes to wash over my face.

'What kind of proof?' His white teeth shine beneath a trendy haircut.

'Oh, man. Thank God you're listening. Listen, this whole thing, this Second Coming, it's staged. It's a hoax. I've been involved from the start. Look at my face, man. They fucking hit me. Look.'

'Who hit you?'

'The ex-FBI guys, man.'

'The what?'

'The ex-FBI guys, man, they're like the head crunches. They're like the fake Jesus' support crew.'

'This is Australia. We don't have an FBI.'

It confuses me momentarily until I understand and laugh, amicably.

'Of course! That's just what we call them, you know, too many American movies.'

'Who calls them that?'

'My friends, man. Well, my ex-friends. I don't think they want to hang out anymore but that's okay because they're bad for me, or I am for them, or we're all bad for each other.'

The suit looks at me without saying a word.

'They took two of us, man, and one of us got away. I mean, neither of us two got away — well, not to start with — but another mate got away, and he was the one who did most of the filming, earlier, when we caught the bastard, and then he got more footage when —'

'Sorry, I'm going to have to interrupt you. What exactly is on the camera?'

Rupert's proud, smiling lunatic face pops into my mind.

'Evidence.'

'Evidence of what?'

'The Second Coming. It's a hoax. We've got it all on camera. We even got him admitting he's an actor.'

'Who?'

'Jesus!' I shout in frustration.

The security guard steps forwards but the trendy guy waves him off.

'Listen,' he says to me. 'You're obviously a little worked up. Perhaps you should come inside and we can have a look at what's on your camera.'

'That sounds grand.'

I enter the foyer, watched on warily by his colleagues, and find myself momentarily stunned by the woman's beauty. Her eyes glitter like ice beneath hair blacker than night; her pillows bulge from the top of her half-open suit jacket.

'Hey,' I say. 'Are you on TV?'

Her eyes narrow.

'Excuse me,' says the young guy. 'Why don't you come this way.'

'Talk to you later, ' I say to the woman as I follow him to the elevator.

The doors close with a ping and we launch upwards. I analyse the back of the guy's blonde, product-clogged hair and wonder if I could do that to myself. If it would make the fox downstairs pay attention to me.

'How about this drought, hey? It's so hot out there.'

'Mm-hmm,' he acknowledges without turning around.

I look down at myself. I'm still wearing board shorts from the beach yesterday, a dusty, vomit-stained T-shirt, and my knees are yellow with paint.

'I must look a real mess, hey?' I say with a loud chuckle.

He turns from his gaze above the door and briefly looks me up and down before returning attention to the floor indicators above.

'You must have been through a lot.'

'Oh, man, you don't know the half of it. This weekend's been insane. They had us tied up out there for the whole night, and then this morning, but then this morning my friend —

'Save it.' The elevator stops and the door opens. 'You can tell us everything in a minute.'

He steps out and I follow him across the floor. It's filled with office recesses and alcoves made out of pin-up board partitions, an organised anti-maze, every cubicle identical and predictable. There are at least 20 partitions, all of them white, all of them empty. Light shines from the windows on one side, making the stations glow like sterilised rectangles under UV, but the whole place is sanitised, even the white-tiled floor is spotless.

'Wow,' I say. 'I've never been on a news floor before. But where is everyone? I thought you guys would be as busy as fuck.'

He stops for a second and looks down his nose at me.

'This building is still under construction,' he says. 'Most of what you see on television is broadcast from our old building.'

He starts moving again and I skip a few times to catch up.

'What do you have left to do? Looks constructed to me.'

We reach the far wall where a single white door is set into its white face.

'Computers. All the computers have to be installed.' The young guy pushes open the door and motion sensing fluorescents flicker into action. It's a bare room with white walls and a round table surrounded by six high-backed office chairs.

'Come in.' His teeth are the same colour as the wall, the door, the white-tiled floor.

'No.'

'Okay,' the young guy says with an impatient twang. 'Why not?'

''Cause where is everyone?' I blurt out. 'There's nobody here. I don't wanna go sit in some room with no one else around on a floor that looks fine to me if you're into offices and shit, but looks like some dead part of Antarctica. This is weird, man. This is bullshit. You ought to be treating me with respect. You shouldn't be looking at me like that. What I've got on this video camera is worth thousands of dollars to you. I could walk straight back out the door and take it to Channel 5, man. How would you like that? Hey?'

'We wouldn't like that at all, Peter.'

'Then take me to your news floor. I don't trust you and I'm not stepping into this fucking room. I'm a victim, man. I'm a hero. I came here for sanctuary, not to be dragged through some sanitised space that reminds of the fucking dentist.'

His white teeth shine back at me with a no-bullshit grin.

'And don't say my name like that. You're not my fucking girlfriend.'

'Okay. What should we call you?'

'Pete.'

'Okay, Pete. Well firstly, we're very grateful that you chose us to show your video to and, secondly, given the events of the past two days and the huge impact it's had on this city, and potentially the world, and given that what you have there could throw a spanner in the works of what people are increasingly calling the Second Coming of Christ, then perhaps, perhaps you can forgive us for erring on the side of caution at this stage.'

He pauses while air conditioning turns the sweat cold on my back.

'Now, I'm sorry if this environment seems a little … isolated for you, but quite frankly, after witnessing your aggression outside only moments ago, it's the best we're going to offer. So please,' he gestures inside the room again, 'take a seat, and my colleague will be here soon.'

'Right.'

I enter the room and sit at the far end of the table, my back to the wall, my face to the door. He remains in the doorway and looks at his watch. The silence quickly becomes awkward. It reminds me of being in detention at school, sitting quietly at my desk with an irate teacher as they mark tests after everybody else has gone home. The minutes go on for hours. The silence is unbearable, yet by the end of the whole ordeal the teacher and I have developed some kind of strange camaraderie, some kind of unspoken understanding after sharing an afternoon's dead air. The next morning they'll give me a personal nod.

'So,' I say, feeling no such camaraderie with this guy. 'Where did you get your suit? Was it expensive?'

He practically jumps with astonishment at the breaking of silence. Then he looks down at his suit.

'Yes, it was expensi —

'What about your hair? Do you get that styled regularly?'

His hands go to his fleece and touch it gingerly, making sure the sprayed hair and gelled tufts manipulated to stand upright in fashionable, bed-hair duplication, remain in position.

'Well, I don't make a habit of —

'How long does it take to do that to yourself every morning?'

He turns to look at me. 'It pays to look well-groomed in this busine —

'Because really, I don't understand it. Girls, yes, but guys? Why the hell do all you tools spend so much time on your looks these days? Do you have any idea how stupid you look? What? You think it's fashionable? Go and get a good hair cut from a barber. Costs fifteen bucks. What'd you spend on that monstrosity? Fifty dollars?'

His lips draw together.

'You think the girls like it? Let me tell you something —

'No, let me tell *you* some —

'No, you let me tell *you* something. Any girl worth their salt isn't gonna go out with a guy who spends an hour every morning doing their make-up. They laugh at you, you know, even that babe with the huge pillows downstairs. Let me guess, you wear pink shirts, collar up, to barbeques too. Right?'

He takes a deep breath, his temper mounting. But then he lets the air out. He wants to be the cool guy.

'Listen, Pete. I don't need to —

'Sheep,' I say.

'Excuse me?'

'Baaaa.'

At that moment the elevator doors open and two men step out. They are much older than Sheep Boy. The one in front looks vaguely familiar and has a haggard face, clean-cut, un-styled hair, and an aura of confidence. The wrinkles in his face have the character of a lion. The second man, overweight and slightly hunched in the shoulders, follows in tow.

Sheep Boy walks hurriedly away to meet them.

'You ought to be taking after that guy,' I call after him. 'Forget your reality shows and Instagram clicks. Your boss keeps it *real*. I can tell already, and by the looks of him, he won't let you suck his cock to get to the top either.'

The leader stops for a moment and looks at Sheep Boy quizzically. Sheep Boy shakes his head and murmurs something before departing in the elevator with the overweight man. The leader steps into my room and holds out his hand.

'About time,' I say, shaking it.

'Yes, sorry about the wait.' He pushes the door so the latch clicks shut with brand new certainty and sits at the opposite side of the table. With the door closed, the walls seem brighter. White like fire, the fluros buzz.

'Now, how much do you want?'

'What?'

'For the tape.'

'For the —

'Tape.'

'But … you haven't even seen it yet.'

He eases back in his seat to regard me, lion eyes clawing over my face, my hand holding the camera, the vomit stains on my T-shirt and finally my eyes. They pierce with self-assurance. They do not waver. They suck at my thoughts. I get the sense he could lean over, open his jaws and swallow everything I know in a second.

'Good,' he says suddenly smiling. 'Let's hear it from the top.'

'But don't you want to see the tape?'

'I would like to hear your story, Peter.'

'Right.'

He looks down at the table waiting for me to begin.

'Okay, but … don't say my name like that. It's Pete.'

'What's the difference?'

My forehead thumps, once, direct centre. But he's not Biddie, even if he does sound strangely familiar.

'Look, Peter. I don't have a lot of time, so let's dispense with the pleasantries. What happened?'

I tell him.

To me it only takes a few minutes but by his body language it must have taken a lot longer. He fidgets, playing with his fingers, analysing the features of the plain, varnished tabletop. He seems bored, increasingly agitated. By the time I finish I feel completely deflated.

'Do you want to see the tape now?' I ask, my voice barely a squeak. 'It's all there. I'm not lying. You can see it for yourself. Here.'

I fumble with the camera, trying to get the little TV screen to flip out.

The Lion leans back in his chair, stretches out long arms to either side, and lets loose a big sigh.

'Tech …' he rumbles with a dry throat before coughing and starting again. 'Technology's amazing these days, isn't it?'

'Whatever,' I say, concentrating on the camera. If the bastard doesn't believe my story, then this footage will get his attention.

'You can create so many illusions, so many stories, so many elaborate events that may not have happened at all, all with the aid of technology.'

I glance up at him as I manage to get the screen to fold out. He's looking at his watch.

'Digital photography, digital TV, digital sound, all of it can be manipulated so easily, spread so quickly through social media. It's hard to know what's real and what isn't these days, really.'

The camera beeps and the screen goes blue.

'And yet, it's that very same technology, even old technology like you've got there, that can shine a spotlight on the most elaborate of hoaxes … by the most unlikely of people.'

I feel him studying me again. I press rewind on the touch-screen buttons and a little mechanism starts crunching inside the camera's casing.

'Shame really. Whoever organised this thing must have spent a *lot* of money putting it together. Have you seen what that little Jesus fella has been doing out there? It could even have fooled me.'

'Did it?' I ask abruptly, meeting his stare with a hard glance of my own.

The digital tape begins to whirr.

'How much do you want for the tape?'

His eyes burn and I drop my gaze.

'I'm not here for the money.'

'I know. You want to expose the whole charade, right? Have your moment of glory and be the guy who brought down a plot to take over the Earth.' He laughs. 'Right?'

'It's just … something I thought I could do.'

'But why not take the money? Are you a fool?'

'I … ' but my throat locks up.

'Peter?'

My left earlobe shudders irritably.

'I said don't call me that. The name's Pete.' My retort hovers over the table for a moment, before circling back and slamming me in the head. 'Hang on a sec. How do you people even know my name?'

The Lion snatches the camera and shoves the table into me. I fall backwards through the fluorescent-lit air, white cylinders swirling haphazardly above my face, until my skull crashes to the floor. The Lion upends the table so it lands sideways on my chest, pinning me to the ground. The door opens, the door shuts, and I hear his muffled voice.

'Alpha Two, Alpha Three. Where the fuck are you? Get here yesterday. We have the camera, time's ticking. Event Four's only five hours away.'

'Bastard,' I shout, hearing the door lock in its well-oiled latch.

'Stay here and keep an eye on that door,' the Lion says to somebody on the other side. 'I'll lock out the elevators to this floor, but if he starts screaming and making noise, go in and knock him out. Got it?'

Somebody grunts a reply.

'Alpha Two, Alpha Three, do you copy?' the Lion repeats, his voice fading as he walks away.

The weight of the table hurts my chest, but I deserve it. Sheep Boy knew my name from the start. I could have walked out right then, but that's the problem with being an antagonistic prick. You're too busy poking people to recognise a trap.

I push, heave and squeeze my body from beneath the table, extricating myself and pushing aside office chairs. I wonder if I could smash the door open with the table but it's painfully heavy. The idea I could lift and move it with enough velocity is laughable.

A group of voices sound from outside. I back up against the far wall as they draw near.

'They had reinforcements, sir. It wasn't just those three. There were two others.'

'Must have been ex-army.'

'Yeah, must have been ex-army. They took us by surprise.'

'You know,' the Lion says as their voices reach the other side of the door, 'when we recruited you lot, we did so with the aim of avoiding complications like this.'

'You've got the camera, haven't you?'

'Dimwit. There are four other people out there, at least, who've been involved in this travesty. What if they backed up the footage? Did you consider that?'

I want to slap myself in the face. How I didn't recognise the Lion's voice from the CB radio is dumbfounding. Biddie's confidence in my stupidity is depressingly accurate.

'Don't reckon they would have got the chance.'

'Jack?' says the leader.

A grunt.

'Go downstairs and see what's on this tape.'

Another grunt.

'Just do it, Jack,' says the Lion. 'And tell Sally to notify Alpha Two that Alpha Three has returned.'

'Now —

'Hey,' I shout, deciding to take a page from Biddie's book. 'If you wanna know where the other guys are, I can tell you.'

Silence greets me from outside the door.

'Seriously. They don't mean anything to me.'

'That's what the other one said.'

'Yeah, and that other one is a bastard and I don't give a damn about him, or the rest,' I say. 'I'll tell you where they are. Just open this door and get me out of here.'

Silence.

'Go in there and find out what he knows,' the Lion says. 'Just get this mess cleared up.'

Footsteps on the tiles trail away towards the lift and I hear the elevator *ping*. It's followed by more silence until, under the boom of my accelerating heart and the drone of the building's air conditioning, I hear whispering. An urgent, secretive discussion is being held on the other side of the door. They're hatching a plan.

I place my hands against the back wall, preparing a plan of my own. I've lied like Biddie. Now it's time to act like Rupert and howl like a dog. Thrash like a fish. Bite like a horse.

The lock in the latch slides back. Fingers creep around the door to push it slowly open.

Letting loose a war cry that strains the tendons of my neck, I launch off the wall, spring off the table edge, and hurl fly through the disinfected air.

Crunch.

My body bounces off the quarter open door, slamming it shut and trapping a set of fingers in the frame. The owner let's out a screech that rattles the wall.

'My finnnngggeeerrs,' he wails.

'Alright alright,' somebody else says. 'Just get out the way.'

Blood oozes from the splayed fingers, staining the perfect white doorframe and walls.

Scarlet upon white, I hate that mix.

Someone scuffles against the door and turns the handle. I pick up a chair, ready to swing, but the handle is released again without the door opening.

'Hurry up,' complains the owner of the broken fingers.

'It's his bloody hand,' says a third voice. 'It's jammed the door.'

'Here, get out the way.'

Somebody slams into the door so it bulges and retracts, but it remains closed. A scream follows. What remains of the victim's fingers curl like withering spider's legs.

'Turn … the … fucking … door handle … first,' the victim pants.

There's a slight pause.

'Good point.'

I return again to the far wall and hold my hands poised against the wall. Howl like a wolf. Pounce like a monkey. Scratch like a cat.

Thud. The door crashes open. A man in black collapses to the floor, clutching his hand. Another man with a bandaged head trips over him. A taller third looms in the door behind his fallen colleagues. His face is black and blue with dried blood from his nose to his neck.

It's Tyson.

'You!' he says.

'Nice face,' I say.

Tyson tries to step into the room but one of the fallen gets up at the same time, knocking Tyson off balance.

'Watch it,' cries the bandaged head. 'My legs, remember?'

'Get up, Bentley, you idiot,' Tyson says, without taking his eyes off me.

I launch off the wall, spring off the table edge, and with an almighty war cry …

My feet land too far over the edge of the table and I slip, crashing into Tyson. He falls against the wall and I land on the two other ex-FBI goons. The one with the busted hand whimpers. The guy with the bandaged head digs into my arm with his nails. Their bodies scuffle as they swear under my body, a twisting mass of octopus limbs that reek of body odour. Tyson, coming at me from above, grabs the back of my T-shirt and pulls me from the mess. He puts me into a headlock, shoving my face into the musty hole of his underarm so sweat swipes across my lips.

 I bite into the webby flesh of his armpit so he shrieks and lets go. I wail. I coil and fall.

'Oof,' says the bandaged head beneath me.

I thrash about, flailing my arms and kicking my legs.

'Shit,' one of them says. 'Where do these lunatics come from?'

A fist comes from above and smashes into my mouth. My wail suffers a hiccup, but I don't stop. I spit the fresh blood from my mouth and shake my head from side to side, creating a broken-tooth fountain of saliva and plasma. They back away in disgust and I'm in the doorway, the whiteness of the room melding with dizzy black to form a broken-glass montage of bruised faces and fluorescent lights. It stops spinning for a moment and I see Tyson and the bandaged head inside ready to attack again. The third lays on the ground, clutching his crippled hand. I lock eyes with him for a moment, air conditioning howling in my ears, then abruptly crush his knuckles with my foot.

He screams.

I back away and run for the elevator. The doors are shut. I head for an adjacent door with a green exit sign above it.

'Get him,' shouts Tyson.

Black shapes hindered by pain lumber after me. I'm suddenly thankful to the Stanleys for breaking their faces.

'I just smash them all up,' repeats the one who wanted to rip out my eyes.

I kick open the door and launch myself down the flights of stairs, yanking the handrails as I turn the corners, leaping several stairs at a time and hitting each landing with a painful compression of my knees. I push my body faster, hurtling down the throat of the building, wishing I could fly weightless through the air as I do in my dreams, as I do when I'm playing vampires, as I do when the fumes of a rich black night extricate me from reality.

I leap again to land on the umpteenth landing but it's harder than the others and my knees give way. I crumble and skid across cool concrete, tumbling like a rag doll thrown. When I get to my knees they scream with pain, but I can't stop. Male vampires are in pursuit. They're no fun at all. And I can see why the floor hurt so much, why this landing didn't give an inch. I've hit the basement where its concrete must lie over solid earth.

I use a railing bolted to the wall to haul myself upwards and limp quickly down a short corridor to another white door with a red-lit sign above it: 'SILENCE'.

Behind me I can hear the lumbering thugs in descent. With any luck they'll head to the foyer. With any luck they won't think to follow me all the way down here.

I push the door open as quietly as I can and enter a white, carpeted corridor with more white doors set into its side. The entrance closes behind me with the quiet suck of soundproofed seals. The sudden lack of noise is unsettling — until I hear raised voices from an open door halfway down corridor.

There's no mistaking his voice this time.

'Jack, I'm telling you we're good,' the Lion says. 'We've got the tape, that idiot's contained, and we'll find out soon enough if they made any copies — although I doubt it. Nobody has this sort of technology laying about anymore.'

'Are you sure of that?' the man called Jack says.

'No, but our boys will get out of him what we need to know.'

'Really, Max? You're gonna torture him now?'

'Not *torture*.'

I want to retreat to the staircase but I can't, not with the ex-FBI goons lumbering about. I creep forward and quietly try the first door to my left. It's locked. I tiptoe to the next for the same result.

'I didn't agree to this,' Jack says.

'What did you agree to? The spruiking of an election gimmick for Family Power?'

'You never said anything about kidnapping people.'

'*They* kidnapped Jesus. Look at the tape.'

I try another door. It's also locked. There's nowhere to go but further into the Lion's den.

'This is getting serious, Max.'

'It was always serious. Do you want to see everything go to hell?'

'Of course not.'

'You know as well as I do that this is the crossroads, Jack, right here, right now. If we don't turn things around, we'll never make it.'

I edge closer to their voices, an accelerating pulse crawling up my throat.

'But we're getting ripped to pieces for political bias on social media, and on Channel 5 and on the bloody ABC.'

'And?'

'You're jeopardising Channel 3's reputation, kidnapping people, hiring mercenaries to —

'They were always going to be a part of this.'

'They're shit. They lost Jesus in the first place. And at the same time as we're faking his Second Coming —

'For one last event, Jack. Just one —

'You're getting photographed having lunch with Tim Carling, for fuck's sake!'

There's one more door ahead of me before light spills from their room onto the corridor's white carpet. I try the handle and, to my surprise, it turns. I slip inside what turns out to be a dark, unoccupied vocal booth. A window into the next room shows the overweight man I saw upstairs sitting with his back to me in front of a number of TV screens. The Lion towers over him with a red face.

'Jack, you've got to see the bigger picture,' he says, his voice now coming through a tannoy speaker above the window.

'We're making the bloody picture!'

'Exactly. *We're* making the picture. This is *our* story. But look what we're facing out there. Less rainfall, less food production, more droughts, more bloody bushfires. There's enough carbon in the atmosphere to ensure shit gets worse before it gets better, no matter what emission targets those lackeys set. *That's* what you should be worrying about, not a few stupid photos on social media.'

I quietly close the door behind me and crouch below the window, my knees shrieking in protest.

'It's not just social media,' Jack says, punching a control button so an ABC TV news report appears on the far wall. It features the Lion in a terse exchange with academic-looking people in front of the Malls Balls — two shiny silver balls sculptured to sit on top of one another in the middle of Rundle Mall. The people's reflections are deformed in the spheres.

'Fuck those boffins,' the Lion snarls. 'We need people to shop. And fuck what they say about Family Power. Tim's got his nose up *our* arse, not the other way around. That's the truth of it.'

'What's truth got to do with any of this?'

'Don't get sanctimonious with me now, Jack. Just turn off that crap and play the damned tape. We need to see if that useless actor identified us.'

I hear the audio scratching of video being played at high speed.

'Honestly, Jack,' the Lion continues. 'We're about to get the highest ratings of our lives, and you want to grow a conscience over a bunch of dropkicks with an early 2000s video camera, for fuck's sake, when … when … what on Earth is that? Is that guy putting his arse in Jesus' face?'

I poke my head above the sill to steal a look. On the TV screens I see Rupert baring his bottom up close to the fake Jesus in the scrub. Our prisoner sits on the ground, tied to a tree trunk, doing his best to turn his bruised face away. Rupert uses both his hands to make his butt cheeks talk. I can hear myself giggling as I film the scene.

'Oooh,' Rupert slurs in a high-pitched voice, moving his cheeks in and out. 'I'm an actor from *Sydney*. I'm soooo good at acting that they made me Jesus.'

'Dimwit,' the Lion says.

'Oooh, but it's so disappointing that we have to film in *Adelaide*.' Rupert pulls up his pants and prances about like a posh praying mantis. 'Nobody ever goes to Adelaide. Not by *choice*.'

A phone rings and the Lion pulls it out of his pocket and answers. He flaps his hand impatiently at Jack. 'Just keep scrolling.'

Jack scrolls through the tape to night time and a shot from inside the car of me swaggering towards a pay phone near a Mitcham bottle-o. Rupert, who must be holding the camera in the back seat of the car, films a close-up of the fake Jesus' face.

'So ... how'd you ... ' Rupert's really drunk now. The fake Jesus, his arms tied behind his back, grimaces and edges away from the camera lens. 'How'd you get into moofies? I could work in moofies. Maybe you could introduce me —

The Lion swears.

'I've got to go upstairs,' he says, hanging up his phone. 'Apparently that guy ... it doesn't matter. Look, Tim's just got here and you and I have to sound like we're on the same page or he's gonna get jittery, okay?'

Jack grunts.

'Okay?'

'Alright.'

'I'll be back in a minute. Just keep going through that shit and look for anything that identifies us. And stop thinking so much. It's not your job.'

The Lion departs, leaving Jack to shake his head and continue scrolling through our tape. I wonder if I shouldn't just stay hidden in this vocal booth until nightfall. But if the Lion's coming back with someone else, there's a chance they'll need this booth. He might even bring the fake Jesus in to record a new miracle.

I peep outside the door in time to see the Lion disappear into the elevator, then slide out the booth and hobble towards the stairs, deciding to make my way to the foyer where I'll make a break for outside.

I listen for the ex-FBI goons as I make my way painfully up the flight of stairs to a door marked with another green-lit exit sign. Stepping through it, I find myself once again in the foyer of the new Channel 3 building where I limp cautiously from a recess in the wall into a bright, high-raftered space. White walls stretch about me. The glass entrance and a desk are at the far end. The Lion and his goons are nowhere to be seen, but behind the desk stands the beautiful woman with black hair.

'Hi again,' I say casually, approaching her desk and the doors beyond. A large widescreen TV flashes with a muted advert for vacuum cleaners on the wall above her. 'How are you?'

'Something wrong with the elevators?' she asks with an emotionally detached voice.

'Nah. The elevators are fine. I just like to use the stairs, you know, to keep fit and all that. What about you?'

The goddess closes her arms beneath her pillows and stares at me impatiently. 'Is there something I can help you with?'

'Well, not here,' I say, leaning on her desk. 'It's a little sterile. But we could go back to yours.'

Like a darting snake, her hand flies down to the desk and hits a button.

'He's here,' she snaps.

Ping goes one of the elevator doors behind me.

'Ah, shit,' I say as I limp away towards the automatic doors. Step, step-step. Step, step-step. Two voices emerge from the opening elevator doors, but it's not the goons, it's the Lion. The other voice is overly loud and nervous-sounding.

'Yes, I think the best thing for us right now is to focus on getting things right. Focus on the future.'

'Forget it,' says the Lion.

I reach the automatic doors but they don't open. They're locked.

'It's never been so imperative that my colleagues and I seize the day, revive morality.'

'I said forget it, Tim.'

'And after meeting that most extraordinary man —

'Tim!'

'Excuse *me*,' the man called Tim splutters with nervous outrage.

'There's no need. That's him. That's Peter.'

'What?'

'The inconvenience!"

'Oh,' says Tim.

'Care to open the door, honey?' I ask the woman behind the desk.

She returns my gaze like a smug vampire, a gorgeous, criminal bitch vixen. It makes her even more attractive. I sigh and face the men standing in the middle of the lobby, the Lion with an intense, agitated frown, the new guy, the loud man called Tim, with an open mouth, looking me up and down with astonished disbelief.

'*That's* Peter?'

'Sally,' calls the Lion to the vampire. 'Get on the blower and get Tyson down here!'

'I already did.'

'*That's* the guy who's been causing all the trouble?' Tim says to the Lion. 'One skinny little runt in dirty clothes?'

'Hey, fuck you,' I say. 'Who do you think you're calling a ... a ... hang on. *You* look familiar too.'

'I don't think so.'

'Yeah, that's right. I *do* know your face. You're on all the election posters. You're that fucking senator from Family Power!'

'What nonsense,' he says, without conviction.

I laugh.

'Peter,' says the Lion.

'Shut up, pig.'

The Lion looks at Tim with a see-what-I-mean-and-isn't-it-a-total-pain-in-the-arse expression on his face.

'You're doing this for an election stunt?' I ask. 'To keep pricks like this in power?'

'If this is Peter,' Tim says, 'Then I think —

'It's Pete, you fucking pigs!' The heat of my scream envelops the entire floor. It's loud, startling, and forces their attention. 'So what you gonna do then? Get everyone pacified, stupefied? And for what? While you guys make a billion? What's the point? I heard you down there. The world's fucked. There's too much carbon, too little effort. So what are you gonna do while you're in charge? Buy up all the water? Hijack what's left of the oil? Smother yourselves with crude mud and toss each other off while we wait for World War Three?'

I spit on the ground.

'Sally,' I call to the girl. 'Even a vampire knows they've gotta keep their crop alive and kicking. What kind of a head vixen are you?'

She scrunches her face with disturbed confusion.

'Pete,' the Lion says, stepping towards me. 'I don't think you're taking the full scale of the situation into consideration.'

'Don't *talk* to him,' Tim says.

'Shut up, Tim.' His eyes bore into my own, assimilating my rage, assimilating my confusion, reading it all in a second. 'It's not just an election stunt. It's a philosophy.'

'Pigs don't have philosophies. They just eat.'

'And you're wrong there too, because it's going to be the people's philosophies, Pete, what they hold onto in the coming decades, that's what's going to prevent your World War Three. Now, let's quit this messing about and —

'Rubbish,' I say, edging backwards towards the automatic doors. 'All they care about is their fucking shopping and their fucking cars and their fucking image and who's fucking outdoor patio looks nicer —

'Exactly.'

' — and self-centred, self-managed, habitat creation in their own little worlds and their own little —

'Peter —

' — nests and financially stable careers and —

'Peter!' he roars.

My sphincter contracts. If this was a jungle, every bird in the bush would flap away squawking in fright; every rodent would leap into the air, have a heart attack and drop dead.

'It's human nature to nest, you little shit.' His eyes are ablaze as he advances towards me. 'Who are you to judge? And it's not just climate change. We're on the verge of overpopulation, fresh water shortages, global disunity and economic collapse. The longer the people stay focused on trivial matters and keep spending, the longer we hold off that collapse, keep things ticking, *maintain* the system in operation. But *you*, you come into *my* building and criticise what we're doing, like you know a damned thing at all. It's not personal wealth we're after. We're giving them hope.'

'Hope,' Tim repeats.

'A reason to endure.'

'God will reward those who endure.'

'We're giving them authority, structure in the difficult-as-hell world of tomorrow.'

'There's no future without faith.'

'Shut up, Tim.'

I back away closer to the locked shut automatic doors.

'Do you believe in God, Peter?' the Lion says, continuing to edge towards me. 'What are you, atheist, agnostic, apathetic? Too woke to contemplate the unknown? The cosmic absurdity of our evolution and self-awareness?'

'I didn't say —

'Even Darwin writes of a Creator breathing life into primordial form. He considered origin of life a puzzle above and beyond his Origin of Species. Who are you to deny the unknown?'

Tim looks at me expectantly. 'Who lit your Big Bang and what did it bang into?'

'I don't fucking know, you arsehole!'

'Exactly,' the Lion sneers. 'Abstract thoughts are useless. But we need it packaged, Peter, a soap opera that's readily consumable. If it's not categorised it doesn't exist, and that's why we'll use Christianity to give them a god.'

'Give them a guarantee,' Tim says.

'A reason to rebuild, to learn from our mistakes, understand our limits.'

'And those who question the word of the Almighty will be crushed with their —

'Tim!' the Lion roars.

' — smart arse memes,' Tim finishes in a wavering voice, retreating a few paces. 'All those damned atheist memes.'

There's a thud and Tyson and Bentley appear through the door at the far end of the lobby. They hobble in bruised and sweaty.

'Where the hell have you been?' The Lion barks. 'Get that little shit!'

'Wait,' I shout, stepping backwards so my palms press against the cold, air-conditioned glass. 'You've forgotten something.'

'Really?' the Lion says. 'And what would that be?'

I hold up my hands in question. 'Where the hell's Sheep Boy?'

'Sheep what?' answers Tim.

I spin around, look above me at the top of the door, spot the green emergency release button, and punch it with one of my upheld arms.

The smooth automatic doors slide silently open.

'Damn you,' shouts the Lion.

'Who's Sheep Boy?' Tim asks.

'I'll get him,' Tyson says, his voice croaky.

'You're fired,' shouts the Lion.

Hot air whacks me in the head like an oven.

I run into a raging earth.

1:43pm

I sprint across the paving, over the manicured garden and towards the road where, as I leap and limp and bound, I see the security guard driving my van into an adjacent car park. I follow it, the yellow, punishing sun reflecting off its tinted windows as it coasts slowly into the lot and stops.

I approach from behind as the driver's door opens and the security guard alights.

'What the …?' he says, trying to turn his head around.

I grab his belt and pull him to the ground, pushing my knee into his neck and ripping his gun from its velcro holster. With a fistful of his hair, I yank the guard's head upwards to thrust the muzzle in his face.

'Where's the fucking keys?'

'In the ignition,' he wails.

Pushing his head back so it cracks into the asphalt, I throw his gun into the bushes and climb into the seat.

'Get out the way or I'll fucking kill you,' I shout, slamming the door and turning the ignition. I back over their corporate garden before putting the van in drive and aiming for the road, aiming for escape.

In the rear-view mirror I can see the Lion, Tim, Tyson and Sally standing out the front of the building watching me, their big red 3 towering above like an icon of worship.

Sally speaks into a handheld radio, and I know somebody's coming after me. This lot could have the entire fucking police force after me for all I know, and I don't have the camera any more. I've no proof of their crime — not that they're going to wait to see what I can prove. They're going to take me back into that white room in that big building, or back out north and put a bullet through my head. After the vampire has had her way, of course. After Sally has sucked the life from me with her perfectly emotionless beauty.

I realise I'm driving nearly 100kph in a 60 zone, and take my foot off the accelerator, breathe, try to think through my options. If I dump the van and lay low for a while I might be okay. They don't know where I live. They only know my name and that's because that little fake prick must have told them. But they do know where Biddie lives, and Biddie will sell me out in a second.

I switch on the CB radio and the voice of Sally with the wonderful-pillows-but-ugly-when-she-frowns face greets me immediately.

' … when subject acquired.'

'Roger that. Why the hell did you let him get away anyway?'

'Alpha Two?'

It's the voice of the Lion.

'Yes, sir?'

'Tyson's fired, as is his entire team, and if you don't bring me that little shit in the next half hour, you can consider yourself fired too.'

Static.

'Roger that.'

'And mark my words, Alpha Two. If that should happen and you do fail me, I'll use the full powers of my organisation to ensure you, your team and your entire outfit, are exposed as having operated in a civilian capacity. I'll air it on the news, on our prime time current affairs program, on everybody's phone. Fuck, we'll even print it in that shitty little newspaper of ours. Got it?'

'Don't worry, sir. We'll catch the bastard.'

'You'd bloody well better.'

'Alpha Two, please report your position,' Sally says.

'Rendezvous with target … thirty seconds.'

'What?' I say aloud.

'Report when target acquired.'

'Roger that.'

How the hell is that possible? I look in my mirrors, but there are no vans, no one driving up close behind me. There's hardly any traffic here at all.

I pick up the mouthpiece.

'Alpha Two, Alpha Two, do you copy?'

Static.

'Alpha Two receiving.'

'Abandon pursuit. I repeat, abandon pursuit. Target is no longer a threat.'

'Sir? I'm not sure I follow.'

'Alpha Two, Alpha Two,' intercepts Sally. 'Ignore last request. Target is on air. I repeat: target is on air. Continue pursuit. Do you copy?'

'Sally,' I say. 'You know, if you didn't frown back there and turn that gorgeous face into a donkey's arse, I think it could have worked.'

Static.

'Alpha Two, do you copy? Please acknowledge.'

'Target in sight. We've got him.'

CRUNCH. The van spins from the impact of a rear-end collision, still travelling forwards, but doing so in reverse so it throws my head against the door with a CRACK.

The van comes to a stop but my vision keeps whizzing, a cross junction spinning, broken glass tinkling, the image of another black van pulling up in front of me, a dented bull bar, figures in black leaping out of the side door. My hand reaches for the ignition. I miss it. Black figures run towards either side of my van. My hand tries again for the ignition key.

Nothing happens, just spinning, just disarray.

I turn my convulsing mind to the gear lever at my side. It sits in blurred drive. Automatics don't start in gear. I whack it upwards a notch to neutral, turning the ignition as black figures reach my door. The engine roars into life. Black figures swear and back away. My foot hits the pedal. I collide with the front of their van and set it spinning. My own van bounces off and finds naked road.

Steam rises from the bonnet in a grey haze that flows over the accelerating van. There's warmth on my neck. It's the warmth of vampire's drool and drips down my bare shoulder.

Lurching mirrors show my assailants back in their van, back in pursuit. But my vision's blurred and shifty. My head's still spinning, heavily. Everything's collapsing and this road's full of cars because I must have changed roads back at the intersection, back where they got me, back where they rammed me, back where they were ready and waiting to 'acquire' me.

I accelerate beyond 90kph, thumping the horn, flashing my high beams, drunkenly pulling up behind slow moving traffic in the fast lane, nudging them aside. I change lanes and overtake on the inside. I change lanes and overtake on the outside. I don't curse. I don't shout abuse. I can only hold on as my body continues to sink sideways, hands gripping the steering wheel for fear I'll lose it altogether. My foot changes from break to accelerator, from accelerator to break. Sometimes it misses them both and tries to rest in lazy emptiness on the floor.

Behind me the other van follows, swerving from one lane to another, honking its horn, flashing its lights, mimicking me, replicating me, gaining on me, and the traffic is getting heavier, tighter, a vice squeezing my head, a wet towel wrapping my legs. I can't get enough speed. The car in front of me will not give way.

The car to my left does not speed up. I'm stuck and blood's pouring down my arm.

CRUNCH. The van slams into my rear and throws me forward so I hit the car in front. It swerves into the left lane, the car in that lane breaking to let them in. I power on to the next car, which sits on 55, oblivious to what's happening, oblivious to me, trapping me in a pack of colourful, happy little cars ignorant of the violence in their midst.

I whip the van out and onto the wrong side of the road, facing oncoming traffic, terrified I could kill somebody. But the oncoming lanes are nearly empty. Everyone seems to be heading south to the city — except that truck.

It flies past with a blare of its air horns.

Except that scooter.

It swerves and drives up onto the footpath with a nasal mosquito beep.

Except that four-wheeled-drive.

A hand flings out with its middle finger extended. The accompanying abuse is thankfully thick as porridge. But drowsiness is layering over me. Warm and wet, it's like an emptying bath trying to suck me under.

Ahead of me an underpass looms. It has sloping concrete pylons on either side to support a pedestrian bridge above. I let the steering wheel slide the van's nose towards one of the angled concrete pylons, a metre-wide ramp that rears upward like a bulwark. I switch on my high beams, rest my hand on the horn and make it scream, a warning to everyone and anyone to get the fuck out the way.

'Shit,' I say to no one in particular.

THUD. It's an impact like a grenade in quicksand — soft but powerful, wet but burning — a shock wave strong enough to vaporise cartilage. My body turns weightless in the air as metal bends, twists, hammers and squeals. Blue skies yawn for a moment, an endless expanse raining with glass until there's a rumble, a long, drawn out grind, hot sparks and screeching metal, and there's no more sky, no more van, no more pursuit, nothing but movement taking my body to a place it shouldn't go, then greyness, the wet slip of something cutting into my head, darkness, the hard feeling of concrete against my chest, then black.

1:54pm

There's no light, no colours, just impenetrable darkness and heat. It licks at my face and smells of burning hair. Surrounding me I can hear crackling fire, hissing steam, vampires feasting in the distance. They growl at each other and fight over shreds of meat.

I want to open my eyes but I'm not sure if they're closed. I'm reluctant to find out. If the mall has fallen and the vampires have won, then it's best to remain in darkness. I don't want to see the end.

Tears well up and slide out skinny. It tells me my eyes are closed. I squeeze them tighter, refusing to acknowledge a city ablaze, orange flames spurting from windows to lick oxygen from the air, spit sparks and send acidic ash to the sky's roof, a ceiling that blisters and bubbles and loses a layer of plastic to fall sizzling upon the carcasses of dead humans.

Intense heat suddenly pokes its tongue up the folds of my shorts and with a cry my eyes wrench open. My leg, under the assault of a sharp little flame burning in a pool of melted goo, shifts away quickly and makes me roll over, makes me roll over again, makes me drive it into the concrete so the flames are suffocated.

It's not as dark as I expected. Hot smoke billows from a burning hulk of metal groaning less than five metres away. And the sky isn't red. The sky is blue. The city isn't burning. The city's going about its business as usual. I'm elevated. I'm on a bridge. I can see the city to my right, small skyscrapers reaching up to the open air where there's no canopy, no darkness, only the acrid stench of burning hair and it's close, *very* close.

Sitting up, I reach a hand to the back of my head. I find hot, crackled, raw skin and when I touch it, when I prod it in bewildered, lingering stupidity, it really fucking *hurts*.

I scream.

There's a shuffle of feet behind me. They are urgent yet they scuff the concrete laboriously. It's a vampire walking through daylight, hindered by the hostile conditions but intent on consuming me anyhow.

I lie back down, roll over and turn my head to see it.

It arrives enveloped in light, the sun behind its head an outer circle, a dazzling ring that withers my eyes. I squint back at the featureless silhouette, sunlight splitting into pyramid shards that pierce the rippling smoke.

'Fuck off,' I say.

'Don't move,' it responds kindly.

What?

Its voice is familiar, beautifully familiar, soft, wise, slightly croaky from age.

'You're injured. Don't move a muscle.'

'It's you.'

'Hang on, hang on. Just stay where you are.'

He steps out of the sun and I'm so jubilant that he's here — and still alive — that I manage to get to my feet.

'I thought you were dead. I thought they took your head.'

'Ah … I'm sorry. I'm a little hard of hearing. But please, just stay still. You're hurt.'

I can see his face now, his grand, old, wonderful face, perfectly wrinkled with years, perfectly toned with experience, full of painful understanding, wisdom and strength. He stands before me, the same height, equal to equal.

Joyously, unashamedly, I step forward and embrace him.

'I'm so happy you're here,' I say into his bony shoulder, tears wetting his flannelette shirt. 'I thought we were done for. I thought it was all over. I thought I was the only one left.'

The sobs flow. My nose empties onto his clothes. I become an upended hose erupting with years of struggle, sadness and heartbreak, and while I do, while I weep like a lost child finally reunited, the Old Man pats my back, the Old Man repeats soothing tones.

'Everything's going to be alright but we've got to get you to hospital. We've got to get someone to look at you.'

'I know,' I say. 'The bastards got me. They were different and they tricked me. They even showed me your head. I thought you were dead.'

I sob into his neck and grip him harder.

'Okay, okay,' he says. 'You've had a nasty hit to the head, son.'

'It's okay,' I sniff. 'The fire singed it and closed the wound.'

The Old Man pushes me back, and looks at my head. I turn so he can see it.

'Oh, dear,' he says. 'You're right. Heavens, we really need to get you to hospital.'

'If you think it's a good idea.'

'Dear boy, I've never seen anything like it. What in the hell happened?'

'Is he alright?' shouts a woman behind us.

'What happened?' says another man.

I turn my head to face them. A couple in their 40s stand on the other side of the burning wreckage.

'It's alright,' I croak. 'But you guys had better get home and lock the doors. The Old Man here is gonna take me to hospital, and if you've got children, you'd better get them home right now. Anything's possible with this lot. They may even be out in daylight.'

They stare wide-eyed. They don't like me, I can tell, but at the same time there's sympathy there. They still want to help.

'Will you be able to manage?' says the woman to the Old Man.

'Yes,' he says over my ear. 'I think it's best if I take him. He's suffered a lot of trauma, and thinks I'm —

'Yeah, no shit,' interrupts the man. 'I saw his van go up the side of the bridge. Bloody hell, it's lucky there was no one up here. They would have been flattened. What the hell were you doing?'

'Doing?' I attempt to bark. 'What was I *doing*? I was trying to save the fucking world, that's what I was *doing*. Can't you see what's happening here? The vampires are taking over the city, man. And I was flying with them. I was gonna stop them, and then ... and then ... a big 3, a great big, red 3, and then it ... and then it ... '

I turn to look at the Old Man. The flickering fire reflects in his grey eyes, shadows from bushy eyebrows leaping about his forehead.

'Just tell them what's going on, please. They don't understand. I've gotta ... I've gotta ... I've gotta sit down.'

A bucket of jelly toppled and spread, I collapse on my knees, which cry in protest.

'Just get me out of here.'

'I think we'd better wait for the police,' says the woman. 'This car could fall down onto the road at any minute.'

'Please,' I say, looking up at the Old Man.

Darkness looms, murky and deepening. Pain is spreading across my entire body, an enveloping pins-and-needles sensation that masks something much worse, something that I can feel rising from the depths like a black submarine. The Old Man supports me by holding onto one of my shoulders.

'Please, just get me out of here.'

My voice is a whisper swirling in an eddy to expand and fly over the city, hissing, resonating, dissipating.

'Don't let them take me. They don't understand.'

His hand slides down to grip my armpit, multiplies into another at my other. Joints creak as he lifts. I do my best to help him but I haven't anything left.

'Please.'

'Okay, son,' says the voice of my saviour. 'But just try to hold on. It's a good thing you're so darned skinny.'

"The following letter was left for me by Peter Mackay on our dining room table approximately three weeks before separation." LT

Why do I spend so much time in Blackwood, you ask, hang out with those WEIRDOS in the forest who drink too much, grow pot, get messed up listening to hippy music and HIP HOP? Truth is, I'm not sure. It's just where I'm from. You're right though. It IS bad for my health.

Last night Rupert threw ROADKILL through the doors of McDonalds and demanded $20 for the meat delivery. Then he pissed in their bin and set off fireworks outside. Today I was back on the flats with you looking at 20 different carpet possibilities, at bird baths, bedroom side tables, brand new kitchens, death by tea towels and INTELLIGENT BATHROOM SOLUTIONS. That trendy radio you bought was the highlight of your weekend. I was more worried about the gunpowder under my fingernails. Then we drove through the city and looked at all the new apartment blocks, the accompanying massage parlours surrounding them like boils, the hipster-themed SMOOTHIE BARS, plastic food DISPLAYS, plastic supermarkets, snap-lock architecture and run-nowhere gym INFESTATIONS. It's like ice-cream pushed through a 3D printer, a clock greased with chip shop oil. It's all gonna melt soon. It's all gonna ignite in a vampire APOCALYPSE. And don't you worry about leafy old Blackwood. It's gonna burn like everywhere else.

Why did I look so sick this morning? Because I feel sick, Leanne. It all makes me sick. Sometimes you do too.

4:25pm

Severe pain changes everything. In that instant a cement truck tips over to land on your legs, all that mattered only moments ago becomes irrelevant. You're mortal, your life's insignificant, and inside your head there's a shining ball of fury.

In your soul.

You cry to the heavens. You plead for the pain to stop, but you're being punished. Every crime you've ever committed suddenly counts. The pain's being handed down personally by God, the Universe, or *It*, *It* which sits as a bursting array of sparks in your shut-eye mind. You're a piece of shit with an ego. Your status as dust floating in an infinite reality is exaggerated. Every particle that's ever collided to give you life will continue to make new muck long after your death, and if you want the pain to stop, you'd better get on your knees and start praying.

Then it passes, the moment of involuntary clarity dissipates as nerve endings become numb, or fireworks of injury settle down into coals, or a doctor shoves a large dose of morphine into your arse. Thoughts of what you should be doing next, or who should be doing what, find their way back and suddenly you are yourself again. Shaken, but not disturbed. Injured, but not being injured. In shock perhaps, but no longer being shocked.

It's here that I find myself now, sitting in a wheelchair wearing only my board shorts, waiting in an emergency room with a green linoleum floor, an intravenous tube extended from one arm to a plastic sack of diluted morphine hanging from a stand, and an old man next to me, allowing himself to be clutched onto by me, held prisoner by me, smiling at me.

'You know?' I say. 'The nature of God, the existence of God, the … *thing* of God, it's … well … it's … '

He continues to smile, his grey eyes watching expectantly. I'm smiling too.

Morphine, it's a wonderful drug.

'Well, it's too bloody hard to explain, that's what it is.'

'I don't think you need to be worrying about such things right now, son.'

'Well, I do. You see ... '

'Yes?'

But it keeps washing away, the pain falls far away. I'm distracted by his face, distracted by his familiarity. I've known him for years. He doesn't need me to explain a thing.

'Well, *you* understand, don't you?' I say.

'Ah, if you're talking about religion and —

'No, I'm talking about *It*, or whatever you want to call it. The God that came *before* religion.'

'I'm not sure I follow.'

Yet his eyes say otherwise. Such depth, such wisdom. He knows what I know. But whatever *It* is rinses out, dissolves into solution, my state of pain progressively less pertinent, progressively less believable, a supreme entity as a force suddenly bright and agonising across my existence becoming a sensation of the past.

'It's a bugger of a thing, though, isn't it?'

'What is? God?'

'You know it. You've gotta work it all out yourself, don't you? I mean, you can try the churches, and there's some good ones out there, but they've got enemies on their own team, people who took God and twisted *It* with business.'

A piece of illuminated glass the size of a coffee table materialises from the dark green lino and rises into the air.

'Sometimes I see people as animals.'

'Wh ... what?'

'And it's not the institutions that are the problem. It's the fuckers who *abuse* them, right? Like pedos at schools, pyros in the fire service. Those places are always gonna be magnets for scumbags, aren't they? And you don't *need* a church to find God, do you? 'Cause there's always the little things, even if you don't notice them at first, even if they don't make any sense. I mean, look at you.'

'Listen, son. You've suffered a nasty hit to the head. You're not thinking straight.'

'I'm not calling you God.'

'I … well that's a relief. But maybe you've had enough of that morphine.'

A nurse walks past to attend to another person sitting on one of a few dozen plastic chairs scattered about the room. The Old Man tries to get her attention. I seize his arm.

'You're like a dad to me,' I say.

'What?'

'I've been dreaming of you my entire life.'

'Of … of me?'

'Yeah, you and me, you've always been in my dreams, in my fights, you're like an angel to me, always at the end when I've won, and look at you now? You're here. You've come and saved me. I could have been burnt to death.'

'Son, it was by coincidence I was at the crash scene, and you pulled yourself from the flames. The ambulance would have been there shortly, but you insisted I take you.'

'Yes, but that would not have been good. They would have got me.'

His brow crinkles. 'Not the … not the *vampires*?'

'No,' I laugh. 'They're just in my dreams.' But now my own forehead crinkles. 'The guys in black, man. *They're* the ones you saved me from.'

'I did?'

'Of course you did. If I had been there a minute longer they would have put a bullet in my head.'

'My Lord,' he says.

'Yeah, maybe. But he's not here now, and that crazy little shit out there sure ain't him.'

'I'm really not sure I follow, Pete.' His grey bushy eyes look up worryingly at the plastic bag of morphine solution.

'You know, that guy out there, the little actress who's prancing around pretending to be Jesus. Don't you watch the news?'

I point to a muted TV screen set high into the adjacent wall where an advertisement displays a smug looking middle-aged couple sitting together on a couch. The man pops open a bottle of sparkling wine and bubbles froth up and spill down its neck.

'Ooh,' says the woman silently — closed captions presenting her words in a box at the bottom of the screen. 'That's got a spark.'

'I know,' the man says with a wry smile. 'I took Viagra.'

'I don't watch the news, son,' the Old Man says as he starts fiddling with my intravenous equipment. 'It all seems a little … excited for me.'

'Exactly. See? We're the same, man. But you're different too. You're an angel from heaven itself.'

'Nurse,' shouts the Old Man. 'I really think this young man needs to see the doctor again.'

She looks up from measuring an obese man's blood pressure on the other side of the room. 'That's why we're all here, isn't it? He seems to be stable for the moment. We all get our turn.'

'And thank God you're here,' I continue. 'I feel better already. I mean, look at that man over there. Normally I'd think he's a pig 'cause he fucking well looks like one, doesn't he? But it's not his fault. His metabolism's just screwed up. Right? And that nurse? Normally I would wanna bend her over that bench as soon as possible. I mean, just look at her fucking pillows. But I don't anymore, see? That would be rude and she's helping people. She's doing something real, right? Just like you and me.'

I pause for a moment, focussing on the glass panel now rotating in mid-air before me.

'Rupert's wrong, man. I'm not a disappointment. I've just felt like I've been fighting the world alone. But I haven't 'cause you're *here*, man. You're here in *real life*.'

I pause again.

'I love you.'

'Oh, boy,' says the Old Man. His bony hand settles on my own to prise it gently from the folds of his shirt. 'Listen, son. I think it's time we called your family.'

'My family?' I ask in surprise.

The glass falls to the floor and shatters silently.

'Yes, son. You're … not okay, Pete. You're not thinking straight. I don't know you. You don't know me, and … we probably need to talk to someone close about your … condition.'

'I don't have any family.'

'You don't?'

'Of course not. They all died when I was little.'

'Oh … I'm sorry.'

'What are you sorry for? *You* didn't do it, did you?'

'Ah —

'Of course you didn't. *That* bastard died too. Stupid driver didn't even see us. I was the only one who survived.'

'Oh, my dear. You poor young man.' He looks across the waiting room to the nurse again, his thoughts turning inwards.

'Don't worry about it. What about you? Have you got any family?'

'I have a daughter. She's married and lives in Melbourne,' he says absently, but his eyes are troubled now.

'See her often?'

'She comes over a couple times a year. She's very busy … I wonder —

'What about your wife?'

'She … ' Finally he turns back to face me, his eyes still hazy with memory. 'Olivia passed away many years ago.'

'I'm sorry.'

'No. It's quite alright, Pete. There's no need. She —

'That's right. 'Cause *I* didn't do it.'

The Old Man regards me for a moment in surprise, and then he smiles, and I smile too. Then he laughs and I laugh too. It's a wonderful feeling, a wonderful sound. I'm sharing a real joke with a real person, and we're not laughing at each other, we're not laughing alongside for differing and opposing reasons, we're laughing together. It fills my heart with joy and I savour it for as long as possible, until my stomach starts feeling queasy.

'Listen,' I say conspiringly as I gaze over the room and the faces inside it.

'Yes?' he says, leaning towards me.

'How are we gonna do it, Old Man? If we're gonna do anything, we've gotta do it now.'

'I don't follow.'

'The fake Jesus. There's an event scheduled for six o'clock. I don't know what it is, but we've gotta be there.'

'Six o'clock? Jesus? Listen, Pete. You're … you're confused, son. I don't think we should be going anywhere. You've got to get medical attention. And it's high time someone saw you properly.'

He glares at the nurse.

'No, it's fine. I feel fine. But really, Old Man, you and me, we've gotta get out there and find out what Event Four is, then we've gotta work out what to do next. 'Cause I haven't got the video tape anymore. They got it. I'm … I'm … '

I slump back in my chair.

'Fucked. Sorry to disappoint you,' I say.

'Disappoint me? Son, I hardly know you. You've just suffered a little trauma, that's all. You're not disappointing anyone.'

'Yes I am,' I say with a morose squeak, tears welling in my eyes. His voice is the reassuring tone of an old friend I never had. A sob escapes my throat. 'I disappoint *myself*.'

There's a moment's silence as I look at the green floor. I feel him studying me. Normally the sense of somebody staring invokes rage but not this time. I want him to study me. I need him to study me. He's the only true sympathiser I've ever had.

'Listen, son. When we leave here, when they've fixed you up, how about, well, why don't you give me a call, hey? Perhaps we can chat when your head's straight.'

'That would be good,' I sob.

He reaches up and ruffles my hair, careful not to touch the burnt wound at the back of my skull.

'You're a good lad,' he says affectionately before returning to look across the floor. 'Boy, if I had grown up without a … ' but he trails off, shaking his head.

'I do have family. *You're* my family.'

'No, son. I'm afraid you've mistaken me for someone else. But I can be your friend, if you like.'

I shake my head, casting aside the sadness.

'But don't you get it? I've been dreaming of you all my life. I'm serious. You've always been here, always in my fights, and always, *always*, we win. And now we've gotta do it for real now. This isn't a dream. This is real.'

'Oh, boy,' he says, a frown creasing his forehead. The nurse pads sternly away towards the emergency room's entrance, traversing the cool, green linoleum purposefully, with direction. Her departure goes unnoticed by my companion.

After a minute, the Old Man speaks again, cautiously.

'Son?'

'Yes.'

Air blows softly out his lips.

'How old were you when … how old were you when … when you … lost your family?'

'Everything's been a loss until now, man. But that's cool, 'cause now you're here. You and me, man, we're gonna change things. We're gonna fuck it all up.'

Air gushes out his mouth until there's none left.

'When you lost your family, Pete. How old were you then?'

'Five. I'd just started school. My Nan looked after me.'

'Your Nan?' he says hopefully.

'She's dead now too.'

'Oh.' And he's lost in thought again.

But I can't wait any longer.

'So are you going to come with me or what?'

'Your Nan …' he repeats to himself, trailing off in contemplation until he nods, satisfied with something in his head. 'Yes, I remember now. They did say something about a relative.'

I sit upright in horror.

'What? Who did? The Bitch? The Lion? The fucking politician? Biddie? Have you met them? Have they been talking to you? I passed out back at the crash. When I woke up I was here. What happened? Did they follow us? Do they know where I live? Are they at my house? My fucking house?'

'Shhhhh,' he says, a father soothing an infant. 'Just calm down. No one talked to me. No one's here. It's just you and me.'

'No one goes near my fucking house, man. No one! I'll fucking kill them. I'll fucking get them and I'll fucking kill them. Tell me. Who talked about a relative? Who talked about my Nan? Who talked about my fucking house? Was it Leanne?'

A bony finger goes to his lips while he sits again in thought. I gape with impatience but manage to hold off any explosion.

'Right. I think I know why you dream of me,' he says.

'God. Why else? But tell me —

'Shhh,' he says again. 'Just listen.'

'Who —

'Please!'

Drool melts like pizza cheese from the corner of my mouth.

'Some years ago, well, many years ago, Olivia and I were in hospital. We had to rush to emergency because she had a, well, a complication, one that ultimately led to her death. But that's not relevant right now. What is relevant is that I waited for them to operate on her, in a room much like this, and while I was waiting —

'No.'

'While I was waiting, the ambulances brought in a —

'Don't do it.'

Black winds suck at my chest, tugging it towards a dark mountain.

'I'm sorry, son, but this is for your own good.'

I already know what's coming next.

'Those ambulances, they brought in a family. It was the saddest sight I've ever witnessed, such a tragedy, such a horrible, senseless tragedy, and amidst all the kafuffle, there was a small boy, a boy with skin the colour of chalk and a look in his eyes that … well, I would remember for all my life. Myself and the boy, we sat in this room while our families were being operated on. I took it upon myself to watch over him. He had no one, only police officers and nurses and … I'm sorry but I just felt so … so … sorry for you, son. I bought you a soft drink.'

I see flashing emergency lights, broken glass under orange street lights, leaking radiator fluid, oxygen masks in ambulances. I see my parents taken away by fast-moving people in hospital frocks, my mother's limp arm, my sister's silent face, placid and white, her eyes closed, the horrible blood smear staining her waxen forehead. Scarlet upon white. I hated it. I hated the shining red muck. I hated its urgency over everything, all of them covered in its filth, all of them motionless, inert, floppy and pale, taken away down the halls. The look in everyone's eyes terrified me. The lingering echo of crunching cars sickened me. I felt like an outcast, a freak left behind with strangers blocking me from following my family. And the nurses all had a repulsive look of fear for me, sympathy and terror mixed together, a nauseating perfume that stifled my breath, made me want to bawl.

But there was a man. A man who didn't follow me around the room, who didn't look at me the same way and whisper, who didn't stink of sympathy and shame. I sat near him and we didn't say a word. He bought me a can of lemonade. It was the sweetest drink I ever drank.

'No,' I cough. 'You're wrong. What year was it?'

'Well, it must have been 1992. No, 1993, Olivia passed away the following year.'

1993. He's right. I was five in 1993.

I slump backwards in my chair, my mouth shutting tight.

'Listen, son. If it makes any difference, I thought of you over the years. You were such a small child. I always wondered what became of you. Such a tragedy. Such a horrible and senseless tragedy.'

Shut up, I want to say. Just shut the hell up. But I don't. I sit quiet with infuriation. My only hope shattered.

'I have to admit,' he adds. 'I'm a little flattered that you remembered me. It seems such a strange coincidence that we've met again after all these years, and in such, well, similar surroundings.' He pauses. 'The world certainly does turn in mysterious —

'Oh, stop it!' I snap. 'There's nothing mysterious about a thing. It's all just … it's all just a pile of messy crap and vague coincidences with no sense to it all and no meaning. Nothing's got anything to answer to. No one's ever going anywhere. Anything can happen to anyone at any time for no fucking reason at all and, at any rate, we're all about to go extinct because in case you haven't noticed, the world's fucked.'

He remains silent.

'And now, now I've been just as stupid as every other pig in this decrepit city, and believed in some kind of … well, some kind of fucking bullshit myself, when all the time, all the time there's been a perfectly rational explanation behind it all, a perfect fucking reason why the only good thing I've ever held onto in my entire life should bother to visit me in my screwed up dreams, and that's just it, isn't it? That's just it. You're just the guy who bought me a fucking soft drink. Ah, fuck it.'

'Pete,' says the Old Man in a soft tone.

I cross my arms and try to block him out.

'You shouldn't swear so freely, and they've been forecasting doom and gloom my entire life, son, for a variety of reasons, but we're all still here. I don't believe it's all that dark or unreasonable at all.' He shakes his head. 'I must admit, I certainly feel a little … spooked, if you will, to be helping you again, to have come across you after another horrible accident. The odds of that are quite remarkable.'

'Bullshit,' I say. 'This city is a tiny shithole. Everyone bumps into everybody here.'

'Mmm, perhaps. But the circumstances?'

I don't want to hear anything more. I don't want to be sitting next to him anymore. I just want to get drunk.

'Well,' he says. 'I'm here for you now and, at the very least, I'm thankful you did recognise me after all these years. I'm getting on, my boy, and the years are taking toll. I didn't even recognise you.'

'Hang on,' I murmur, sitting up.

'Just … take it easy, Pete. Just because you can't feel the pain, it doesn't mean you're not hurting. I'm right here.'

'That's right. You *are* right here. I've been dreaming of you for as long as I can remember, and now you're here, in the flesh. But how come, right? How come in my dreams, you always appear as the old man you are now, and not the younger man you were back then? Hey? What about *that*?'

'Well, gee, son. That *is* interesting. Are you sure?'

'Absolutely. Without any doubt. Exactly like you are now. Never any different. Always like this. Always this old. I didn't even remember you from back then until you brought it up, and please, don't ever do that again.'

'Well, it's like I said,' he says after a pause. 'The world *does* turn in mysterious ways.'

At that moment, a door crashes open and two silhouettes stand at the entrance, the late afternoon sunlight outside casting shadows on the corridor before them.

I turn quickly to the Old Man. 'Are you gonna help me or what?'

'With what?' He follows my gaze to their elongated shapes on the green linoleum floor. 'Are they the … the people who wanted to shoot you?'

'Vampires. I need you to help me now, Old Man.'

'Wh … wh …' he stammers, finally unnerved. 'What do you want me to do? I really do think you should stay here and wait until —

'Look,' I say, getting shakily to my feet. 'You know it, and so do I, that you and I have some kind of … well, some kind of connection. I don't understand it, but it's there. Right?'

'Pete. Please sit down.'

'Give me your telephone number.'

'Now?'

'Hurry.'

The Old Man fumbles around in his breast pocket and produces a short pencil that looks older than me, and a carefully folded piece of blank paper.

I keep an eye on the distending, advancing shadows, which pause to talk to the triage nurse in the admittance booth, then reach up and unhook the morphine sack from the stand.

'Thank you,' I say, holding out my right hand. 'It was great to finally meet you … again.'

'Well … certainly,' he says with confusion, handing me his number and shaking my hand.

'When all this is over, I'll call you and we can get together for a … well, for a coffee, I think. That would be sensible.'

'Pete, I really don't think you're in any condition to go anywhere. Nothing's going to happen to you here. It's a hospital, and besides …' he hesitates before adding with determination, 'I won't let it. You've suffered enough.'

'Thanks, but this isn't about me. Those guys down there, they're gonna be ex-FBI goons, and when they find me, they're gonna ask a whole heap of questions and make me suffer, and by then it will be too late.'

'Too late for what?'

'Too late to save the pigs from their own slop.' I let go of his hand and step backwards. 'When those bastards come, tell them I went to the bathroom, down that way.'

I point to the doors next to us at the edge of the room.

'But your injuries.' The Old Man's eyes plead with me to sit back down. 'You can't.'

'I'll be fine,' I say, shaking the quarter-full bag. 'I have morphine.'

He looks at the drug with horror.

I turn and start walking away towards a little alcove on the other side of the room where I'll be hidden from the entrance corridor.

'But Pete!' the Old Man exclaims, doing so with an urgent, high-pitched whispering.

I lift my arm and wave at this man of my dreams, a comrade in arms against a shopping mall world of vampires. Seconds later the guys in black walk emerge from the corridor, led by the nurse. They pass me unknowingly and make their way to the Old Man's bewildered face. I step out the alcove, sneak behind them, turn the corner into the corridor, and crawl beneath the admittance booth window. Then I stand up and head drunkenly away from them all, back towards the double doors of the emergency entrance, back towards the afternoon sunlight and a battle I'm starting to wonder if my entire life's been cultured to fight.

I only hope they leave the Old Man's head intact.

"The following letter was left for me by Peter Mackay on our dining room table approximately one month before separation." LT

Dear Leanne

They call this the City of Churches. That's funny. The only time I go to churches is for funerals. Seeya Mum. Bye Dad. Farewell little Sis. Goodbye Nan. I don't think this is the City of Churches. I think it's the City of FUNERAL PARLOURS, the City of People Who Drink Too Much, like me, according to you. But what else can a guy do here? Award-winning booze is everywhere. The Barossa, Clare Valley, McLaren Vale, this place can't get enough of its award-winning DEPRESSANT. You say there's more than booze. You say there's beaches, clean beaches, needle-free sand and shit-free water. That's true. But there's also SHARKS, real big motherfuckers, but that's okay 'cause they're like mosquitos. Enough booze in your blood and they'll bite once and spit you out, right? What about sports, you say. What about cricket, football, and sailing? Sailing? Sure. Maybe I'll also go bicycle riding with the yuppies, dress up in lycra and ride in the middle of the ROAD. Maybe I'll invite them all over for a barbecue and we'll compare coffee grinders, outdoor kitchens, lay bets on who's gonna die from

cancer first. I'll join their club and
CONSUME, buy designer clothes, designer
sunglasses, buy a Range Rover and go
shopping, buy a labradoodle, hang out in
parks with yummy mummies, complain about
kids on Snapchat, post pictures of kids on
Facebook, wrap my designer dog shit in a
PLASTIC BAG and invite everyone over for
WINE'O'CLOCK.

You smell so nice. Your perfume makes me
stable. I'd like to come home later, rest
upon your pillows, try not to fart beer from
ten hours of abuse. But you hate me when I'm
drunk. You turn your head like I DISGUST
you, like I smell like DEATH. I probably do.
Mosquitos won't have me either. Sorry if I
STINK but this is the City of ALCOHOLICS.
I'm stuck here with the rest of the pigs and
at least the booze stops me screaming.

It's Friday night and I'm heading out.
Maybe I'll see you later. Maybe I won't.

4:58pm

I duck and weave out of the hospital emergency entrance, stagger down concrete access roads, climb and fall over concrete balustrades. I make my way to the Flinders Medical Centre bus exchange, all the time holding my intravenous gear aloft, all the time conscious of the sight I must present: half naked, half burnt, half-a-head-of-hair.

When I reach the bus stops I see a used newspaper on a bench. There's a picture of the fake Jesus under a front page headline: 'Who in God's name is this?', and then in smaller type at the bottom of the page, 'Follow on Facebook', 'Tweet if you see Him'.

I ask a small group of teenagers staring at their phones if they believe in omnipresent intelligence.

'What about religion? They're not one and the same, you know. Words, titles, and appearances mean fuck all. Look at me. I used to hate you, but now I don't.'

The teenagers stop sniggering and stare.

'It's true. I've changed and you can change too. You wanna find God — and you can call it whatever you like, but I reckon it's easier than saying *It* — then first you've gotta trust it. You've gotta let go. There's a lot of things you just don't know.'

The teenagers back away. I follow them.

'Or maybe break a leg, snap an arm, half kill yourself in a car crash. It worked for me. I felt *small,* man, I felt *It.* 'Cause it's not about some church at the end of the world, it's between you and *It.* Fuck, saying *It* is too hard. You use the damn word for everything. Call it the Universe, or God, or Buddha. You can even call it Bob, if you like. Bob doesn't care.'

They turn and walk away.

'Abstract thoughts are useless,' repeats the Lion in my head.

'Excuse me,' somebody says next to me. I turn around to see a guy about my own age smiling with lips that seem unhappy about it. 'You look like you've had a tough day.'

'What of it?' I say. His cautious eyes stare guiltlessly into my own. 'Can I help you?

'Oh, you don't need to worry about me,' he says. 'I just wanted to tell you that, well, something wonderful has happened.'

'It has?'

'Yes, and rather than explain it to you when you're kind of already, well, you know. I would just like to say that at six o'clock today —

My ears prick up.

'Yes?'

'At six o'clock today something else wonderful is going to happen.'

'Where?'

'At the Bay, near the jetty —

'Always the small things,' I say with a thankful nod.

'What? Well, yes, I guess, and do you know who's going to —

At that moment a bus packed heavy with people arrives and crawls to a stop.

'Jesus,' I hear the guy finish under its thunderous tones.

'Not today,' I say, approaching the opening doors, instinctively aware that my fate lies within its guts. I step on board and realise I don't have a wallet. Somewhere in the events of the weekend it abandoned me. But before I can think of an excuse for the bus driver, I'm throttled with the sound of talking, jabbering, laughing and giggling, an excited crowd on its way to the town fair.

'So many people,' I murmur to the bus driver.

'Mate, it's been like this all day. You wanna step out of the door-well?'

'I haven't got any money,' but my voice is far away.

'Looks like you've had a hard enough time already. But hurry up. I'm behind schedule.'

I shuffle onwards into the throng — confused, stoned, dazed by their pastel colours. They're wearing pinks, yellows and oranges, but then there's a lot of blue too, collared shirts with swirling insignias at their pillows and breasts reading 'Power and Life'. A woman gets up from her seat for me and smiles. 'Rest, you poor man. You're going to the right place.'

'Jesus will heal you,' says a little kid in the seat behind her.

'I'll hold onto that for you,' says the guy who spoke to me at the bus stop, standing behind me in the aisle. He takes my near-empty plastic bag of morphine as I sit down.

The bus accelerates out of the hospital bay. Kids behind me cheer.

'I would have thought more people would get on board from here,' some lady says. 'Such faith, this young man has. There should be more.'

'There will be,' a middle-aged man in a blue shirt says. 'Mark my words. This is only the beginning.'

They nod and congratulate and smile at me while the late afternoon sun beams inside to throw shadows and shapes over their features.

My head is suddenly pushed forward by an invisible force.

'Ewww!' cries a small boy.

'Don't touch it, Samuel,' says a mother's sweetly chastising voice. 'Leave the poor man alone.'

I turn around to see the boy behind me holding his forefinger out. A tiny piece of crispy flesh from the back of my burnt head is stuck to his nail.

'Sorry,' says his mother. 'Samuel is just a little … curious.'

I smile at Samuel. He doesn't like it and shakes his finger hurriedly. The piece of meat flings away to land among the travellers.

'Don't worry about it,' I say. 'I can't even feel it.'

'Really?' he asks sceptically.

'Morphine, kid.' I point to the plastic tube travelling from my arm to the near-empty bag held aloft by the bus stop guy. 'It's a wonderful drug.'

I nod to his mother, smiling. She smiles back, but it's not the same as before. There's a glimmer of anxiety beneath her slightly painted lips.

I turn to face the front and concentrate on the passing houses, suburbs, shopfronts and warehouses. People walk their dogs. Couples hold hands. Shiny-roofed cars putter here and there, turn down side roads towards homes where dinners will be cooking, parents will be humming, families will be settling in to feast together and talk about their days.

Leanne wanted such a dream, a husband and kids, a house they could call their own. She wanted it with me. I tried to crush that idea, kill it with my darkening heart, but she wouldn't give up.

I remember coming home in a mood from hell one afternoon shortly after we split. I'd been out all night, having crashed in the subterranean lair of a dope-smoking chick who played hard metal at full volume when we fucked. She tasted like resin. Her pillows were small and hard. It was my first foray into singledom and I didn't enjoy it at all.

Leanne's package lay waiting on the doorstep. There was no return address on its back, just 'PETER' written in black. I took it inside, feeling lost, feeling sick, even lamenting Leanne as I was unaccustomed to being by myself, especially with a hangover. She was always good at nursing me through such self-inflicted misery.

She seemed to enjoy it and that morning I missed her. That morning I felt sick for pushing her out.

I took the unknown parcel to my lounge room and sat down. Ten minutes later, having scraped my catatonic eyes off the ceiling, I opened it, taking a full thirty seconds to slide the gummed paper apart with my keys.

There was a photograph frame inside. It was an old photograph, one I knew well, and one I hadn't seen for many years.

The picture of my family showed we were happy, all of us smiling, all of us proud. One boy, pleased as punch, one slightly younger girl, her eyes still a little red from having cried only minutes before when I hit her for the first and only time in my life. My parents stood behind us, holding us both, cherishing us both, loving us both.

The next day they were all gone.

There was a little yellow post-it note stuck to the corner. It was Leanne's writing:

'Thought you might want to keep this.'

Seconds later I was weeping, broken, lost, guilty black winds assailing me. I felt stupid, pathetic, damned. Perhaps Leanne did know something about me. Perhaps she wasn't so blind to my condition. Perhaps she was the best friend I ever had.

I called her, clutching the picture frame, snot dripping from my nose, and when she answered, I couldn't talk. But Leanne could. She soothed me. She warmed me. She felt as confident as a person consoling another in grief can always be, and she *had* me. She'd broken through to me. She'd pulled me back from the darkness.

'Maybe … ' I started.

'Yes?' she said, a nervous hope in her voice.

'Perhaps … '

'Take your time, honey.' Her voice oozed through the plastic headpiece of Nan's old landline.

Heat twitches within the cavities of my kneecaps.

But then something fell from the picture frame, something that had been fastened to its back with Blue-Tac. It was a picture of Leanne, captured in a park shortly after she'd had her hair done, a selfie she'd texted me three months ago, and one she'd apparently had printed to send me again. It was, I suppose, her last ditch attempt to get through to me, to salvage our relationship, but its inclusion reiterated everything about her I didn't like.

It was still all about her.

Worse. She'd ripped out a heartbreaking photo of my lost family — a photo I'd deliberately hidden away — to exploit its potency and penetrate my barriers, make me cry, and then added *herself* to the frame, stuck her own face onto its blade, all in the hope I would think of *her* as my heart is chopped to pieces, consider *her* my new family as I'm destroyed with the old.

My neck buzzes with discomfit.

'Peter?' Leanne asked through the plastic phone, still savouring her moment, still anticipating the words that would bring her back into Nan's house as a partner and a willing, taxing appendage. 'What did you want to say?'

'You're a cow,' I finally whispered.

'What?'

'I said you're a fucking cow!'

'Peter!' she wailed. 'How can you say —

'Because you nearly had me.'

'What do you mean?'

My knees are no longer just warm. They're smouldering. My neck is no longer just uncomfortable. It's aching.

'I said you nearly fucking had me!'

And Nan's phone flew across the hallway, smashing into pieces I would repair two days later when I finally returned to my house, *my* fucking house that the selfish woman would never step into again for as long as I lived. Then I went out, got exceedingly drunk, and screwed a fat chick with the biggest fucking pillows I could find.

'Fuck!' I scream on the yellow bus of happiness, culling the crowd's incessant nattering. They look at me in shock. The dickhead standing next to me holding my bag of drugs frowns.

'Give that bloody thing a squeeze,' I shout.

Startled, he fumbles and drops the morphine sack.

'It's empty,' says the kid behind me. 'I saw it all go.'

'What?' I say, attempting to turn around and face the little shit. But the action is excruciating. My neck's made of reptilian skin pulled too tight. I can't help but scream again.

The kid starts crying. His mother pulls his head into her bosom. Stunned believers cover their mouths with their hands. One of them gives me a shrewd stare and shakes his head. The bus driver makes a right turn so it lurches over a gutter, sending everyone swaying and grasping onto yellow poles or each other. My half-turned neck bumps against my collar bone, twists my head further with the bus motion, sends my hot face in a near 180-degree turn to lock eyes with the kid's mother, and it hurts. It hurts so very much.

'Faaaark!'

Standing passengers back away. Others in the aisle make space for them. A shrivelled old woman with a tea towel over her head crosses her fingers into a crucifix and hisses in my direction.

'Devil,' someone says.

'Just leave us alone,' says a different mother holding one of at least ten hollering children.

'Wait,' shouts the guy I met at the bus stop, still standing next to me. 'He's just a guy in pain. He's run out of morphine.'

'Look at his skin,' someone else says. 'It's burnt.'

'Like the devil.'

'He's from hell itself.'

But the guy doesn't listen. He leans towards me, holding out a smartphone to my eyes.

'Look,' he says, motioning to his phone's display. 'This was recorded yesterday.'

I manage to turn my head around so it rights itself with my torso. The ensuing scream is louder than my first.

'Look,' the guy repeats, unflustered. 'It's Jesus. He can help you.'

I look at his screen and see the fake Jesus standing in a fruit shop, helping a man get to his feet from a wheelchair. A news reporter holding a bright red Channel 3 microphone speaks enthusiastically in the foreground. A crowd of onlookers stand about in awe. But it's wrong. The fruit shop has an open front and outside it's daylight, hot, bright, wickedly dry daylight.

'Yesterday?' I ask the guy.

'Yes,' he nods. 'He just walked into a fruit shop yesterday afternoon and starting healing people.'

'Yesterday?' I ask again, a little louder.

A middle-aged man in a blue shirt nods at me, worriedly.

'Are you fucking serious?'

My shout ripples through the busload of nitwits and gullible gits. Multiple crosses are shoved in my direction, some created with fingers, others within necklaces complete with tiny sculptures of Jesus Christ nailed in crucifixion. Several smartphones hover among them recording me, documenting me.

'I hate you,' the boy screams from behind me, whipping his head out of his mother's pillows before shoving it back in.

'It's not possible. Yesterday I had the bastard tied to my mate's smashed-up car in the middle of the fucking hills, in the scrub, right up until nightfall. Before that I had him knocked out cold in the boot of a car from the moment he arrived at the beach, and you want to tell me that footage happened yesterday? What are you? A bunch of fucking farm animals?'

'Just get off this bus,' demands the middle-aged blue-shirt man, stepping forward.

'Sure,' I reply. 'Gladly. Just tell me, do any of you have something to drink? Something really fucking strong? 'Cause I tell ya, I'm in a lot of pain here and could really do with a good hit or 10 of Scotch — I mean whiskey. Any goers?'

The bus lurches to a stop. Everyone sways forward and grabs onto something or someone.

'This is your stop,' says the man. 'Now get off.'

'And go back to the hospital,' says the mother clutching her brat of a kid.

'And go back to hell,' adds the old woman from beneath her tea towel.

I blink.

'Okay people,' booms a different voice from the front of the bus. 'This is the end of the line.'

Chattering starts again en masse and they rush for the exit, trampling what's left of my intravenous gear on the aisle floor, every kick tugging at the needle in my arm, pulling the tube further from my skin.

THUD — something whacks the back of my head, creating a mass of blue dots that splatter and regroup to implode in my vision, sending icy white sewing needles from my scalp to cover me in a patchwork quilt of razor sharp, motorised, twitching metal fragments.

'Hey,' says the mother of my assailant.

'But he's the devil, Mum.'

All I know is agony. All I know is I want it to stop. All I know is I am calling out for God again as the floor of the world rushes up to greet me once more.

5:35pm

An endless void of isolation and stardust piles into me from a million light years away. It collects bits of my soul, bits of my life, memories of everyone and anything I ever knew, before passing through to travel a million more.

The few tender moments I had as a child in my loving mother's arms — gone, useless, a billion galaxies from me. The few happy moments I had with friends before we became wasted shadows — gone, useless, everyone forgotten and on their own way to oblivion. The tender moments I had with Leanne when we were still innocent students at university — gone, useless, everything and everyone dismantled.

My limbs extend a thousand miles. My face stretches flat across the universe, an oval kite pierced by electrons. What's left of my soul remains compressed in a black hole, frozen with pain and despair for the certainty that no one gets out of here alive. This is where we are all headed and nothing, *nothing* makes a damned difference at all.

What's the difference what's the difference what's the difference?

Hands grab me. Strong hands, grasping hands, they find parts of my body rotating in localised vortexes and twist them with precision, grapple with sadism. They have the body odour of rotting dinosaurs and the universe is growing dimmer. The certainty of everlasting nothingness dissipates into pins and needles and then … and then …

I smell something else for a second, a familiar second, before I'm suddenly aware of straight Scotch being poured directly down my throat.

My eyes snap open to see a vaguely familiar face hovering before me, accompanied by another less familiar and older face.

'More,' I say.

More comes, burning spirits of fire, but in comparison to all I suffer, as cool as the cucumber slices Leanne used to put on her face.

Shapes and colours come into focus around me.

'More.'

'Don't you think —

'More!'

I guzzle and swallow, wishing the hot fluid could be inserted straight into my gut.

'Hold on, this stuff isn't cheap, you know.'

'More.'

Spirits flow, my stomach grows warm but not horribly so. It's the warmth of imminent intoxication, not of second-degree burns.

'You're gonna be drunk,' warns the voice of a young guy, a familiar guy, a guy who held my drug sack and showed me pre-recorded footage of his fake saviour healing a fake cripple.

I take the bottle from his hand and upend its contents into my mouth.

'Bloody hell,' says the other face with a uniform on, a face that gave me a free ride on his happy bus of hellish freaks and which now flags a body that reeks.

Bus drivers so often do.

The bottle grows light in my hand. I retrieve it from my mouth, wipe my tingling lips, and hand it back.

'Thanks,' I say, before slumping into a heap and closing my eyes. 'My name's Pete.'

A hand shakes my shoulder.

'Hey, you've got to get up. Jesus will heal you.'

I open my eyes.

'Oh, yes, that old chestnut.' The bus interior swells and begins to spin in that oh-so-familiar spin. 'I've got news for you, my little duck.' And he is a duck, a happy cartoon-faced duck. His earnest eyes, his well-brushed hair, so innocent, so concerned. 'Your Jesus is a fake.'

'What?'

'Yep.' I close my eyes again, sleep beckoning, pain receding like a tide. 'The whole thing is a hoax.'

'You've gotta get that guy off my bus.'

'But you're wrong,' Duck says. 'He came out of the sea. He can heal you.'

I reopen my eyes and there are two of him. Two ducks, two sincere gazes, four bodies taking on the motion of everything else to bypass my eyes on a carousel.

'Were you there?'

'No, but —

'I was. I saw the whole thing. Then I bashed and kidnapped the bastard.'

'That doesn't make any sense.'

'Come on, get off the bus now. Before he pukes. I'm heading to the city.'

'Mall,' I correct him.

'You're wrong,' Duck says as he wedges his arms beneath my own and lifts me to my feet.

'Ow!'

'I'll show you.'

The bus driver points us towards the side door, his face dripping with the spin of his blue-yellow bus pole world. I glimpse the quarter-full whiskey bottle hanging from his hand.

'I need this,' I say, taking it off him.

'You … oh, whatever. Enjoy it.'

I hold my finger in the air to make a point I've already forgotten. Seconds later I'm pushed down the steps by my new associate. The doors hiss shut, the bus engine roars, and the whole yellow mess lurches away to reveal a sight that confuses me entirely.

It's a crowd, a large, noisy, banner-waving crowd of thousands that begins across the road and spreads over the entire paved area of Glenelg's Moseley Square. Beyond them the beach and jetty are empty because everyone's here, standing before a three-story building at the square's far side, gazing up at a stage set up on its roof, blue fabric signs reading 'Family Power' laying limp on either side, an empty address podium complete with a microphone and PA system between two vertical placards. It resembles the instruments of superstar rock bands before the musicians appear, inanimate yet primed for action.

'This is Event Four?' I mumble to Duck.

'C'mon,' he says, pushing one of my shoulders to get me across the road to join the cacophony.

I take a swig from the bottle, holding rigid against Duck's persistence. I look at the peoples' faces, open-mouthed, shouting, yelping, crying. Some of them have joyful, childish tears running from their faces. Others clutch their pillows and erratically hop from one foot to the next. I look at their clothes, colourful, pink, yellow, flowery orange. It's an assembly of colourful playschool presenters, trendy modernites, women in cleavage-revealing pastels, blokes with dyed, product-filled hair, old people standing here and there like forgotten ghouls. Pocketed among them in groups of four or five are people wearing the same blue shirts as those on the bus.

Duck succeeds in pushing me across the road so I stumble and drop the bottle.

'Wait,' I say.

'C'mon,' he says, pushing me firmly, getting me onto the other side where we enter the crowd, where quieter ones stand in spacious, fragmented groups on its outskirts. Their watchful faces stare at the rooftop, completely ignorant of me and Duck. They don't even notice when I step on their toes, bump drunkenly off balance into their backs, claw my way through their throng. There's too much noise, too many lungs sucking air, and somewhere further in there's chanting. Repetitive, aggressive, it rocks my abused head. I can't hear what it says but it sounds anxious. And there are too many faces. Hundreds of gaping mouths black and moist inside, wet or wide-open eyes, all gazing up at the roof at the far edge of the crowd, a fleshy mash-up that gets progressively denser at Duck's incessant pushing.

'You've got to get to the front, so he can see you.'

The air grows hot with human heat as we advance on the centre. The chanting gets louder. Breathing is difficult. Pain lurks beneath my skin. I need to piss. Bile is rising. I can feel it coming. I need to … vomit.

A dizzying array of concrete and feet one minute, a haphazard mural of beer, Scotch and carrots the next, I kneel on the ground and expel the poison from its larder like an elephant shitting. But as I claw for breath in-between convulsions, staring at the growing sludge through tearful eyes, I begin to regret my stomach's failing. It's brought a little sense back to my head. My nerves are re-awakening, agony is re-emerging, and the act of vomiting has further aggravated my injuries.

'Ow,' I squeak, looking up with watering eyes at a small pocket of colourful people looking down at me with disgust, one or two crying for real as they flick bits of puke off their shins.

A man-sized chicken pushes through the crowd to stand over my head and cluck angrily. I blink the water from my eyes.

'Get out of here,' he squawks.

'No, leave him,' Duck says, coming to my assistance again. 'Can't you see he's sick? He's the one who needs to be here the most. Look at him.'

Pain is bubbling and creeping back up the beach. I'm no longer smashed — curse my weak stomach — just nicely toasted. The tide of feeling is fast advancing, threatening to shatter what little tolerance I have left, and when it does, I'll be finished.

Duck lifts me to my feet and I hold on with two crispy baked arms.

'Duck. Go back to the road and get my bottle. Whatever's left, I don't care. Just get it. Get me some booze, quick.'

'Bloody alcoholic,' someone calls.

'Fuck off,' I scream, whipping my head around to look at the bastard. He has the head of donkey and turns his long muzzle sideways to stare at me with one white-rimmed eye.

'Eeee-awww,' he brays.

I lurch away but it hurts. It hurts so very, very much.

Duck pulls my shoulders, leads me further into the crowd where the chants get louder and more boisterous by the second. He shouts into my ears.

'Just hold on, Pete. You're nearly there. It's six o'clock now. Why would Jesus be late?'

'Duck, you stupid son of a bitch.'

But I'm too crippled to resist his incessant direction. He takes us deeper, parting shoulders, backs, beautiful women and cosmetic boys.

'Please.'

'Nearly there.'

'I need help, Duck. I need a drink. I can't do this like this. My head's going to fall off.'

'Almost there.'

'My skin's coming off. My knees are going to break open. I'm injured, Duck. I need a drink.'

'You won't be in pain much longer, Pete. I promise you.'

'It's not true. Why won't you listen to me?'

But Duck doesn't listen. Duck's on a mission.

'Here. We're nearly at the front!'

The people are no longer colourful. They're all wearing blue shirts. They all have 'Power and Life' stamped on their right pillow — and there are a lot of pillows. There are a lot of pretty 20 year olds, well-groomed teenagers, happy little kids. There are middle-aged glamour ewes, tanned rams in fogged-up glasses, but there are no old people. This patch has a demographic of 3 to 40. There's no room for the aged. All must be beautiful. All must have perfect skin and well-groomed fleeces. It's here that the chanting is in full force. It comes from their guts: 'Power! Power! Power!' over and over and over again. It *is* a rock concert. It *is* a stadium buzzing with pre-performance electricity. These sheep bought their tickets months ago.

'Duck,' I shout, but he can't hear me over the herd. We're stuck right near the front and I may as well be a fly on somebody's rump.

'Duck,' I scream, but he's transfixed like everybody else.

'Power! Power! Power!' Duck chants, his eyes glued to the rooftop directly above us, the underside of his sweaty white neck shining in my face.

I reach out and slap him across his cheek.

He looks back at me with astonishment, rubbing his skin.

'Why …?' he begins, but then the crowd erupts with hyper-applause. The place rumbles like an earthquake, and Duck returns his gaze to the roof.

A man in a blue shirt stands at the edge, looking down upon the crowd, arms held out.

'Ladies and gentlemen,' Tim the Politician says.

His amplified voice is ear-splittingly loud. It ricochets across the quadrangle and the heads of the crowd, across the public square and probably down to the beach as well.

'There's been some technical difficulties. But Jesus is here now, waiting in the wings, and he'll address you shortly.'

The crowd responds joyously, shrieking and clapping before organising itself into chanting once more.

'Jesus! Jesus! Jesus! Jesus!'

I watch the smiling Tim with loathing and see something else I recognise, a TV crew, a camera set up to one side of the stage with a great big, bright red 3 on its side.

Six o'clock. Just in time for the evening news.

I shake Duck's shoulders, trying to ignore the pain it wreaks upon my own.

'See, Duck. Look. It's them. It's the bastards who set this up. Look at them.'

But Duck's one with the mob and nothing will break their focus.

It suddenly surges forward, pulverising me, shrieking, clapping and stomping.

Jesus has arrived.

He skips quickly across the roof towards the stage, his white frock billowing behind him like a cape. The jostling crowd swarms and crushes each other. I push backwards at those driving me forward, while the bastard, the little actress prick, reaches the podium, steps up to the microphone stand, and smashes it violently to the side so it crashes out of sight with a feedback whine.

It sends the crowd even wilder. I almost expect him to pick up a guitar and start playing it behind his head, but instead he extends his arms over the crowd, just like Tim the Politician, and speaks with a voice that carries with the same amplification even without the microphone.

'People, I have no need for manmade contraptions. Can you hear my voice?'

Everyone screams. Everyone answers tumultuously in the positive.

'I said: Can you hear ... my ... voice?'

I want to put my hands to my head, such is the magnitude of the uproar, but my arms are pinned to my sides, my body wedged in amongst a crowd of crazed penguins.

'Then watch, my people, watch and witness the power of God in all His might.'

Crackling white fire blows out the front of the building. Sparkling gold shoots over our heads from the edge of the square. We cover our faces. We close our eyes from the burning powder, and when we return our gaze to the roof, Jesus is no longer standing. Jesus is levitating, hovering above the podium like a circus performer, arms outstretched, his white frock shining fiercely, smoke from the fireworks obscuring his features, masking him in a haze that makes us cough and wipe soot from our eyes.

'Children, I have returned. I have come back from heaven with a message for you all.'

The crowd shrieks hysterically and I feel utterly powerless, utterly crushed, utterly trapped in the clutches of mobocracy. Jesus' smoky face shifts colours, alters texture. It contorts into a rippling montage of indiscernible shapes. On either side of the podium, blue fire swells from behind the posters, sending shadows over his multicoloured body, accentuating his eyes as two otherworldly pits of furious black.

'I … have … a … message! And you had better heed my message, for those who ignore the will of God will forever suffer.'

'What is your message?' wails a voice from the crowd.

'Tell us, Jesus.'

'We'll do whatever you say.'

It's difficult to breathe. There's no air, no space, just a chaotic, oxygen-sucking mob, and the pain, the agony, the heat in my exhausted being. I look for Duck but he's two people away from me, stuck in the crowd like me, yet completely ignorant of anything other than what's floating above, what's holding everyone in command.

'Duck,' I yelp over the racket. 'Help me, please.'

'And it is my will that you spread this message,' the fake Jesus says. 'It is your duty, every one of you here and every one of you watching today with your earthly technology. Because what I say today, must be passed on to generations across the world.'

'Duck,' but I know it's useless. I can't compete with a dazzling spectre issuing orders to all humanity.

I wrench my hands out from the pit and over my head with a scream. I'd collapse to the ground if it were possible. But I'm propped upright with people on every side of me, leaving my arms to flail above like an upside down octopus. They crumple over the head of a young woman in front of me, inadvertently brushing her pillows in descent.

She twists around to look at me with accusing eyes.

'Sorry. I didn't mean to. I'm just in so much pain.'

'Pig!'

She slaps my face, a sharp *clap* that draws people's attention away from the fake Jesus, gets them looking between me and the girl, registering the fact she's in a blue T-shirt and I'm wearing nothing but shorts. Somebody shoves me. Somebody spits at me. The immediate crowd diverts its energy towards us and I'm moving, finally, we are all surging, heaving, a raging wave pitching towards the stone face of the building.

'People,' bellows the fake Jesus. 'My message is this.'

I'm slammed against the wall where protruding rockface sandstone scratches my skin. Somebody shoves my head and blue dots appear in my vision. A hoof presses my face against stone.

'Tell us, Jesus,' squeals a voice from the crowd.

'Tell us your message,' brays another from the turmoil.

I see a door set in the wall five metres to my right. The door is closed. The door is blocked. A guy stands in its shadow, a familiar shape in black.

Tyson.

I thought he was fired. But our eyes lock as he speaks into a walkie-talkie. I push back against my assailants in the crowd's front line. They respond by pushing me again.

'Why don't you listen to Jesus?' I scream at them.

The effort makes me dizzy. The crowd's too dense and Tyson's on the move. He's making his way towards me, edging against the wall, sliding between the crowd and sandstone like a spider.

Blue dots grow large and dark in my vision, bobbing and swirling like balloons. Among them the Old Man's head appears, decapitated yet alive.

He smiles. He nods.

'I'm really not sure I follow,' says his voice from the hospital.

Tyson shoves a blue-shirted model away from the wall. He's only three metres from me. I can see the injuries on his face.

'And you will listen now, as if your ears have never heard before,' the fake Jesus says.

Whatever animal was pushing my face against the wall finally lets go and my head drops to my chest with a snap.

'Yes! Please, yes!' bleats a monstrous ram near my ears.

Unconsciousness beckons. I welcome its blackness, waiting for its delicious nothingness to submerge me entirely. But cursed hands lift my head upright again.

'Pete.'

'I failed, Old Man. I can't do this. Just leave me.'

'No, Pete!'

'For too long you have let the unqualified, the unholy, run your lives. They have brought war and sickness to your inheritance, your earth.'

'Can't stop it, Old Man. I'm done for. It hurts too much and it's too noisy. I give up. I want to go now.'

'No, Pete. It's me.' Skinny fingers poke into my eyelids and force them open.

Duck's sweaty red face is inches from my own.

'Leave me, Duck. I'm done for. Let the vampires have their way.'

Dark blue everything.

'You have let your ego and thirst for knowledge poison the water. You have allowed it to take precedence over God.'

'Pete ... hey. What the? ... Hey, get off of me. Pete!'

Opening my eyes, straining dizzily against the fury of swimming oblivion, I see Duck grappling with a spider, the rest of the crowd hindering their efforts in a mesh of limbs, chants and perspiring brows.

My eyes close again.

'You have let those who know nothing of Grace convince you of the power of information, of ambition.'

'And it's high time someone saw you properly,' says the Old Man's dismembered head in front of my face. It dematerialises to reveal a vaguely familiar face anchored to a slightly hunchbacked, overweight body.

'Peter,' says Jack from Channel 3.

I flinch as the sweaty man puts his arms on my shoulders and turns me towards the building.

'You can climb this.' He points at the wall, a shimmering rampart in the late winter sun. It seems to grow and sharpen before my eyes. 'You can climb it and put an end to this freak show. I'll boost you to the first window.'

'Pete,' Duck quacks again. I look back and see him wrestling hopelessly with Tyson.

'Hurry, Peter,' Jack says, his face having transformed into the Old Man's again. 'Climb.'

'It's Pete,' I say wearily. 'But alright. Just 'cause you were real, Old Man. Just 'cause you were real.'

'Only *God* is knowledge. Only *God* is truth.'

I step onto the Old Man's interlocked hands and allow him to boost me up the wall, reaching one hand to the top ridge of a sandstone brick. I raise my other hand to a brick higher up.

'Go, Pete. Go and see Jesus. He will heal —

Duck's last words are deafened with a thud.

Stepping on the heads and shoulders of the people beneath me, I claw my way up the stonework.

'Hey.'

'Get off.'

'Pull him down.'

'Climb,' shouts Jack.

'People,' continues the bellowing voice above from within his plumes of smoke. 'For too long you have allowed my church to be questioned, debated and ridiculed, abandoned by the ministers of governance.'

I ascend beyond the grappling hands of the crowd and the reach of Tyson who now stands directly beneath me. He drops his walkie-talkie, grapples onto the jutting sandstones of the wall and prepares to haul himself after me.

'This is why you are lost.'

I find a window ledge at the peak of my reach. But my feet slip and slide over the pieces of stone, unable to find purchase, unable to find leverage. My fingers alone don't have the strength to pull me up.

'This is where you have failed, where you have walked from light and allowed darkness and despair to rule.'

Tyson surges upwards but, in doing so, puts his head within reach of my foot. I step onto it and leap. He falls crashing back into the crowd. I pivot my body in the air so my butt comes down upon the windowsill.

'But the church must not be neglected. Intellectualism cannot be idolised.'

I rest upon the ledge in excruciating pain, looking downwards as Tyson recovers and gazes upwards into my eyes, glaring at me, hating me, a tarantula closing in for the kill, a predator sent half mad through starvation and drought. His fingers claw once more for purchase upon the wall and I prepare to move again. I have to. Vampires are merciless.

'People. This … is … my … message.'

I reach my burning arms to the top of the window frame and stand on the ledge, my crippled knees seemingly splintered within.

'People. My *church* … must … *be* … your … government.'

The crowd roars, a terrible zenith that hits like brick. I can't help but look down at the crazed core of people beneath me, all wearing identical blue shirts and hollering at the figure above. Surrounding them are people in regular clothes, some standing about talking excitedly to each other, most of them with a phone in hand that they use to take selfies from time. Still further away, on the crowd's outskirts at the edge of the square, a hundred or so people pace about shouting aggressively at the crowd. They film with their own phones as well.

I feel myself swaying, moving with a sea of faces, invisible carbon bubbling from open mouths to accost the earth, the atmosphere, a cluster of parasites at odds with their host. I could fall backwards into their mesmerising uselessness and disappear but hugging the wall directly beneath me with four black-enclosed limbs is a bruised face, teeth grit with detestation, angry blood leaking from his nose where my latest efforts to fend him off have made him even angrier.

I reach above the top ledge of the window bay, taking hold of my new handhold before jumping and twisting, swinging my legs about to sit down upon a higher zone of rest at the top of the window.

'I give you now the first of my new disciples. He will prove to be wise in my absence for I cannot stay long upon earth.'

Catching my breath, trying in vain to concentrate on anything other than the outrage of my screaming limbs, I realise the fake Jesus' voice is no longer amplified. My climb has taken me above the projection of whatever sound system is at work. His voice is small, just like in the sand dunes, just like in the scrub, and his attempts to sound commanding is pitiful.

'Don't go, Jesus,' I hear a voice shout from the commotion below.

I look at what remains of my climb. The roof sits barely a metre-and-a-half above this top ledge. I get to my feet and find I can even see over it.

'You must listen to my disciple now, people, for he knows the details of my plan, and there is a plan, people, a wonderful plan, one that will usher in a new era of prosperity.'

The fake Jesus has returned from his spectacular flight to stand upon the podium. From here I can see the wires. I can see the carabineer poking out from a hidden harness at his waist. People wearing black are hidden in the alcoves of an adjoining building standing several floors higher than this one, their leather gloves handling thin wire from a pulley system hooked four metres above the stage, all of it obscured from the crowd by Family Power banners and lingering smoke.

Tim the Politician steps out of shadows at the edge of the podium, a salesperson smile on his lips. He picks up the microphone stand, jogs quickly onto the stage, and resets it to the thunderous applause of the minions. On the far side of the stage I see a Channel 3 camera crew recording the scene and, in the shadows behind them, I see *him*, the yellow-toothed Lion watching from the wings, observing everything, a puppet master present to ensure his show runs fluidly.

He barks into a walkie-talkie, his eyes red with anger, his mouth animated and furious. He's probably calling for Tyson.

Tyson!

I whip my head around just in time to see the spider lunge for my leg. I kick at his hand, sweeping it away, but momentum brings his face into my foot.

Tyson's nose breaks with a distinct crack. He regards me with revulsion, a brief snarl, which morphs quickly into dread as he realises he's about to fall backwards — from three stories in the air.

His fall chokes the throng off in an instant. Seconds later bodies are crushed and bones break. I can hear them cracking in the crowd's sudden, abhorrent silence.

Does it matter if I didn't mean to kill him?

Somebody screams.

'Thank you,' says Tim the Politician, his amplified voice bouncing off the heads of stunned onlookers. 'Firstly, I would just like to reiterate how … well, how amazing all this —

'Murderer,' yells a woman from somewhere three stories below.

'Ah … excuse me?' says Tim, bewildered.

'Stop him.'

'There's a dead man down here.'

Agitation ripples through the mob. I hoist myself over the roof's edge, tumbling upon the flat summit before getting to my feet.

'Bastard,' hisses the Lion's unmistakable venom from across the rooftop.

Tim backs off the podium aghast. The fake Jesus lowers his outstretched hands, his face swathed in fear. I can see lumps of makeup hiding the bruises on his face.

'Don't stop,' orders the Lion in the shadows.

Tim backs further away as I stride towards the podium. He stumbles over a cable and the microphone stand topples once more. Feedback squeals across the quadrangle. The fake Jesus clutches his left ear in pain, before managing an unconvincing, wavering smile for the turbulent mass watching below.

'Speak,' growls the Lion.

'People … ' the fake Jesus begins, but his voice creates more feedback.

'Fuck,' says the Lion.

I climb onto the podium and bend down to pick up Tim's microphone stand. A flying shoe whizzes past my head. I reset the stand but another shoe slams into my chest.

'Fuck!'

The crowd gasps again.

'Don't be such a bunch of arseholes,' my amplified voice echoes across the square.

'Cut his microphone, for Christ's sake.'

'Yes, sir,' shouts a man from somewhere.

'This isn't Jesus,' I shout into the microphone. 'He's a fucking actor from Sydney.'

Shoes launch, sandwiches fly, cans of Coke spin through the sky spurting trails of black sugar. I try to dodge the missiles but take a half-eaten hotdog to the ribs, a splash of sweet liquid across my face.

'Stop,' the fake Jesus pleads, cowering.

The projectiles cease immediately.

'Now take control, you little shit,' the Lion says. 'Tim. Get your fucking arse back over there.'

'This isn't what I agreed to.'

'Well *I* can't do anything, can I? They can't see *me*.'

'What difference does it make?'

'Dimwit.'

'Fireworks? Smoke?' I shout. 'What the hell is wrong with you —

My voice returns to a normal volume. The microphone has been cut.

'Finally,' roars the Lion. 'Now, get Jesus back in the air. And more smoke. Dimwits! Set off more fireworks.'

'Roger that, sir.'

The fake Jesus suddenly lurches as the slack from his fly-wire is taken up. Fireworks burst about us. Multicolour sparks drive into my bare skin but I can hardly feel them. It seems my nerves are burnt to cinders. But the fake Jesus can. He yelps and buries his face into his arms as his rises into the air, a petrified rag doll shaking at the bottom of a fishing line.

'See,' I shout. 'It's bullshit.'

But the crowd can't hear me. Fireworks are continuing to pop, the sky is filling with smoke, and beyond the plumes I see the Lion mustering his black ex-FBI goons, readying them to 'acquire' me.

Police sirens sound in the distance with high-pitched urgency that cuts through the racket. It's at once relieving and terrifying because now I'm a murderer too.

Does it matter if I didn't know she was married?

'No,' I shout. 'It's not ending this way.'

The Lion's grin flashes through the smoke. Yes it is, it says.

'No, it's not.'

I turn to the fake Jesus, now hovering half a metre above the ground, now balancing his weight for the fly-wire, now stretching his frocked arms to either side.

Fuck it.

I take a short run up, leap through the air, and latch onto him.

'Oof,' he says.

The momentum sends us careering on his wire, swinging in a semicircle over the stage and across the roof, colliding into a TV camera to send it clattering and whizzing inches past the Lion's face. There's a *crack* as the short crane supporting our wire buckles with the sudden weight, breaking out to emerge from behind the Family Power banners that obscured it. It shudders in a squeal of twisting metal and popping bolts, and suddenly the fake Jesus and I are sent over the roof edge. He hangs from the small harness around his waist. I hang onto the carabineer at his back with one hand, the other hooked desperately around his hips, both our legs dangling with flailing absurdity three stories over a crowd of shocked people in blue shirts.

I can smell the fake Jesus' perfume. It stinks of flowers.

The crane cracks again. We plunge about a metre on our wire, jolting with the impact as it halts once more, my hand in the carabineer almost becoming dislocated in the process.

'Help,' the fake Jesus screams, his voice loud and amplified. A flesh coloured earpiece sits nestled in the fake Jesus' ear. I begin to pull myself up his body.

'Don't,' he screams in terror. 'Just stay still, you crazy fucking arsehole.'

The crowd begins to shout again.

'What's happening?' yells a frightened voice from below.

'It's a hoax,' shouts another with pseudo outrage.

'Fucking fanatics,' screams a dissenter among them. 'You're in on their hoax!'

Shoes start flying again, but this time not just at me, at the stage beyond us, at Tim the Politician, at the blue-shirts gaping upwards with angry eyes.

I put my foot down upon the carabineer at the fake Jesus' back, holding onto the wire that stretches up to the hapless crane six metres above our heads. I reach down to the fake Jesus' ear and yank out his earpiece, holding it aloft to the crowd.

'See,' I shout, but it's not necessary. The ear-piece microphone is acutely sensitive and my voice thunders from the speakers. 'What did I tell you? The whole thing's a fucking joke.'

A half empty tub of yoghurt splats into my chest.

'Will you stop throwing things!'

'Oh, God,' moans the fake Jesus as he's pulverised in a flurry of food, shoes and rubbish.

A cheeseburger slams into my hand holding the wire above my head.

'You fucking —

The unshackled crane drops again, sharply. We plummet through the air and the crowd beneath us recoils, until the wire jerks to a stop once more. It leaves us stranded about three metres below the rooftop level and ten metres above the ground.

The fake Jesus begins to cry.

My palm holding the wire has split with friction burn but I still can't feel anything over the fire in my skin. And at least the crowd has stopped throwing things for a moment. Police cars and an ambulance pull up on the road beyond the crowd. Cops disembark and form a barricade around the mob. A Channel 5 TV crew films from outside it.

'Help,' the fake Jesus yelps.

I slap his head.

'Leave him alone,' shouts a blue-shirt beneath me.

'Shut up, you stupid bastard,' yells another man.

He's stupid?

My forehead swells.

'*He's* stupid?'

I feel my throat constrict with frustration.

'You're *all* fucking stupid,' I scream into the fake Jesus' earpiece. 'You're all a bunch of fucking farm animals.'

'Get stuffed,' shouts a woman beneath us.

'It wasn't our fault,' a whining voice calls.

'Wasn't your fault? Wha? … Of course it's your fault. It's all our fucking faults. We're a bunch of shopping mall sluts, branded fucking penguins. Don't you get it? They did this 'cause they *can*.'

'Who are you to speak to us like that?' rebukes the well-to-do voice of another blue-shirt as the projectiles fly.

'Who am I? I'm Jack Shit. That's who I am. But at least I've got the sense to work that out. But you lot … you're farm animals. Get some fucking balls, the lot of you.'

'Fuck you,' someone screams.

'Would the person hanging from the crane, please calm down?' pleads a tinny voice through a megaphone.

'Get this crazy man off of me,' screams the fake Jesus.

'It wasn't our fault,' the whining voice persists. 'We *need* a miracle.'

'Just calm dow —

'Miracle? Mira … what the fuck?' My forehead splits apart and ants cascade down my face, latch onto my tongue. 'You selfish fucks! Why don't you act like *intelligent* pigs for a day, stop shopping and clean up your own fucking mess? That would be the miracle. Shit it might even save our arses. Fuck, you might even become worthy of a real Jesus then.' But once again, the microphone's cut off, my final words lost to noisy, outraged air.

'They're gonna burn you, mate,' I whisper into the fake Jesus' ear. 'When you get out of here, they're gonna burn you, you and your cronies.'

But the fake Jesus is ignoring me to look upwards at the roof. He shakes his head frantically, terror in his eyes.

'What?'

I follow his gaze to the roof and meet the eyes of a lion. They glow, preparing for a kill. Smoke swirls about his face as a cameraman appears alongside to point a Channel 3 lens down at us from over the roof edge.

'Well, shit,' I say to the fake Jesus. 'Now I'm in your story too. Now we're both fucked.'

The Lion turns his back to the crowd and runs a finger horizontally across his neck.

A new siren hollers from the square. I turn to see a fire engine making its way slowly through the crowd, honking its horn, burping its siren, doing its best to disperse a reluctant horde. A ladder begins rising from its roof.

'Hurry,' screams the fake Jesus.

I grip onto the wire and begin to haul myself up.

'Stay still,' bellows the megaphone.

'Stop moving,' pleads the fake Jesus.

'We've gotta move, now!'

But the wire is too thin to climb and my tormented body is weak.

'Sir, you've got to stay still. Help is on its way.'

'Stay still, you fucking fool,' shrieks the fake Jesus as my efforts cause us to swing from side to side, drawing a few creaks from the crane above.

'There's no time,' I say. 'Put your arms above your head and start climbing the wire.'

'I can't do that, you nutter. You'll kill us both.'

I try again to hoist my weak frame up the single string ladder, my hands bleeding, my knees swollen and numb, but it's useless. I turn to look at the fire engine's progress and see the ladder already extended, the truck crawling through the final rows of stubborn onlookers recording us with their smartphones, and in my fingers on the wire, through the pain of distressed skin, I feel vibration. Somebody's tampering with the wire at the other end.

'Hurry,' I scream. But it's too late. I know it's too late.

'Swing,' I shout to the fake Jesus. 'You've got to swing us closer to the wall.'

'They're nearly here.'

The fire ladder's barely a metre away from the fake Jesus' floundering feet. He stretches one of his legs to its advancing tip. He nearly reaches it, but not quite, and the exertions send us shaking backwards towards the wall, wobbling about like skewered chickens on a stretched slinky spring.

Crack.

The wire lets go and we fall.

The tip of the ladder snares the fake Jesus' leg and his body spins to crash beneath its angled frame, toppling him in a full-length somersault before velocity pulls his leg free and sends him plunging to the pavement below. I come down hard onto the top of the ladder, smashing feet first into one of the rungs, twisting, crunching, my own leg catching to break my fall. The rest of me continues to swing downwards until my head crashes against aluminium rungs, my spine bending backwards until an electric bolt engulfs me with a *snap*. I'm left swaying upside down in mid-air, my broken leg caught in the ladder, my neck flopping downwards with the weight of my head, my eyes blinking as I try to make sense of a waving, pulsating, upended horizon.

The fake Jesus lies arms outstretched on the pavement, legs together and toes pointed in a final, desperate act. Blood wells from his crown in a scarlet halo.

To his left lays the much less picturesque heap of Tyson, his blood already dried on a pavement still hot from the day's drought-inducing, skin cancer-producing, sunlight hell-bent on bringing humanity to its knees.

And now I sense my own body disengaging from the ladder, shifting a little but stopping again. Something is holding it up. I want to see what it is but I can't move my head. I can't do or feel anything. All I can do is imagine a piece of my shinbone sticking upright to prevent my leg from slipping through the rungs.

Just let it go, I will to the travesty.

It does.

My body slides loose from the ladder and I fall.

Everything is silent — except the thoughts in my head:

'You wait till you're about to die, man, then you'll start believing,' Rupert says. 'You'll start praying like every other chicken shit in this world.'

But he's wrong. I don't need fear of death to find reason. It's been here all along.

'Such a tragedy, such a horrible and senseless tragedy,' the Old Man says.

He's wrong too. There's no tragedy here, just training to thwart a crime written years ago, a pawn designed to suffer so when the battle came he was ready. Now I've done what I was meant to do. Now I can go home.

'Take your time, honey,' Leanne says.

Time's up, darling. You can keep the house and you should know, you were right for me. It wasn't your fault and you were right. Now stay the fuck away from me forever.

Asphalt looms. I glimpse the fake Jesus' blood spread about his brown hair, red ink, pale white death.

I hope I'm about to join my family.

I know that I am.

I hope I'll get a chance to apologise to my sister.

I know that I will.

White fabric shoots up to my face, covers my eyes with an impact harder than life.

'Are you sorry, Peter?'

His voice hits my soul with infinite depth, the thunder of all and everything that's ever been and will. A tear emerges and I experience a moment of truth I never could have found alone.

Father, I was never anything else.

6:17pm

A thousand years later and after travelling one thousand back, I'm awoken by the sound of a camera lens rotating in short, violent movements. I open my eyes to the reflection of a contorted body. Next to it stands what would be a pretty woman if her glossy make-up didn't shine like plastic-wrap. She stares wide-eyed at me, unsure what to do, her blue Channel 5 microphone forgotten as I stare back.

The camera operator alongside her sniffs violently every few seconds as he pushes the lens closer to my face. They loiter in the sunset sky until two upside down men in green paramedic outfits arrive and push them aside.

'Don't move him,' says one of them, crouching at my chest.

'His neck looks broken,' says the second.

'Just … don't move him.'

'I think his arm is dislocated … his leg … Shit, look at his back.'

Beyond them I hear a murmuring crowd, police ordering people to stay back, sirens in the distance, angry shouts from a rooftop.

'He's awake,' says the Channel 5 woman, leaning over the paramedics with her cameraman. 'He's looking at me.'

'What's your name?' asks the first paramedic. 'Can you move your fingers?'

I smile at the reporter. The cameraman sniffs again, adjusts his focus.

'We should probably get the deceased from out beneath him,' the second paramedic says.

'Just … don't move him,' says the first, peering into my eyes.

'Try to frame the dead guy out of it or we won't be able to go to air,' the reporter says to her colleague. 'What's your name?'

I hear my sister giggle in the distance, imagining the winds of a cool change lifting the plastic from the reporter's face, blowing it away, dispersing everything fake so it scatters like dust into a universe that never really needed our names anyway.

'Peter. What's yours?'

Special thanks to Arts South Australia, Patrick Allington, Amy Doughty, Daniel Keane, Adrian Riggs, Kate Shaw, Gemma Opie, Jordan Noblett, Steve Dyson, Sara Porzio and my family. Thanks also to Heath Riggs, Mike Sexton, Ben Brennan and Martin Cooney.